RISE, KRAKEN!
ALEX LAYBOURNE

SEVERED PRESS
Hobart Tasmania

RISE, KRAKEN!

This is for my wife Patty and our five wonderful children, James, Logan, Ashleigh, Damon and Riley.

CHAPTER 1

June 18th, 1952

At seven years old, Forrest Jones learned that monsters existed in the world. At seven years of age, Forrest Jones became an orphan. At seven years of age, Forrest Jones first tasted another man's blood. At seven years of age, poor Forrest Jones became a man.

The sun beat down upon the tourists like a death ray. Forrest heard them talking about the unseasonably high temperatures, even June. The sky offered no respite from the incessant beat down of heat. Forrest didn't care. Kids are carefree. With the sand beneath his feet and the sea stretching out before him, Forrest was happy. It could have been ten degrees hotter, and he still would have loved every minute of it.

The Cuban weather was nothing but another fantastic memory that a young boy should be able to cherish forever.

Playing on the beach right by their hotel, his father was away organizing something, a surprise he had said. Forrest loved surprises. Forrest and his mother waited patiently, just the two of them and a grand expanse of beach. Sunning herself, content watching her son play, Forrest's mother smiled and waved. Forrest waved back and ran into the ocean. The warm water was so cool against his sun-soaked skin. He dove beneath the surface and the world fell away.

Forrest loved the water. The waves and raw unbridled power of the ocean fascinated him. Even as a baby, his eyes would fall on the pictures of the sea and they would hover there, as if he could feel the pull of the tide even through works of art.

Breaking the surface, Forrest swam. A good, strong swimmer, many claimed him to be a natural talent in the water. He splashed and jumped in the ocean, the innocence of his youth still surrounding him like a protective veil.

"Forrest, Forrest, come here, son." He heard his father's joyful voice calling him. He saw the smile on his face and could not pull himself out of the water fast enough.

Like any kid of his age, Forrest idolized his fair share of heroes. George Reeves's Man of Steel was a favourite of his, yet above them all, stood his father. Arnold Jones was his son's biggest hero. His dad worked hard. He did not understand what he did, but he knew that his father's job involved money. He worked in a bank, not where people put their money, but in an office. A big office. Forrest spent a lot of time there. Everybody treated him special.

Yet above being a hard worker, Arnold Jones was a devoted father. He did everything with his son, his every waking moment, when not at work, he spent with his only child. The apple of his eye. Arnold was a man who believed in discipline, and would punish Forrest for doing wrong, but he raised a good boy. A boy who listened to the rules.

"What do you have there, father?" Forrest asked, eyeing the papers his father held in his fist.

"Son, I have booked us a sailing trip. We are going to sail for the day, around the islands and out into the ocean. We are going to have an adventure." Arnold beamed ear to ear.

"Really?" Forrest could not contain his excitement and nearly leapt into his father's arms.

"'Yes, the captain of his yacht says that we can sail the ocean and find any adventure we want. He knows all of the islands, big and small. What do you say?" Arnold asked his son.

"When do we leave?" Forrest asked excitedly.

"Tomorrow morning. Just the three of us." Arnold kissed his wife, who had gotten to her feet.

"I don't know, darling. I'm not a fan of boats. I don't want to be a bore," Evelyn spoke.

"Nonsense. You would never be a bore to us, would she, Forrest?"

"Uh-uh," Forrest proclaimed and then proceeded to run back towards the ocean.

That was the beginning of the end. Forrest turned back and waved at his parents. Little did he know that he would never again have the chance to see them standing together, arm in arm, as always.

CHAPTER 2

Early the next morning, Captain Faizon Arnaz waved them down and offered enthusiastic greetings. He welcomed them on board his yacht, the *Santa Maria*, a Bermudan Sloop with a beautiful blue and red paint scheme. The rich colour of her wooden deck and the brilliant white of her sails as they caught the early morning sun.

"Welcome to the Santa Maria," the captain spoke. He was an older man, with dark brown, sun-creased skin. To Forrest, it looked like leather.

"Thanks for having us," Evelyn spoke.

"My pleasure, ma'am. We have a great day ahead of us. Clear skies and smooth seas. We should be able to visit a few islands, take a stroll around. Maybe even a swim. I bet you would like that, young man, wouldn't you?" The captain crouched down to look Forrest in the eyes.

"Yes sir, I would. I love the water." Forrest smiled and nodded.

"I can tell. The ocean calls to us. She is a mighty fine lady, and she either accepts us or rejects us. One thing is for sure, once she gets into your blood, her call cannot be ignored. Let me tell you though, you need to respect the ocean. She is our mistress, and those of us that are lucky enough are allowed to spend our time in her company."

The boat cut a smooth line through the water, the wind filling the sail, which billowed outward, pushing the boat faster through the smooth ocean.

Forrest was taken by Captain Arnaz. He found himself fascinated by the man, studying everything he did as he controlled the ship and steered them out into open waters.

All around them islands dotted the horizon offering a visually stunning array of sights. The warmth of the sun and the freedom of the ocean infected them all. Even Evelyn had a smile on her face as she sat arm in arm with her husband.

The first island they stopped at was a tiny, unpopulated place. A paradise on earth to the city-born and raised Forrest. He ran through the rolling sand-covered dunes and hid in the shadows of the tall palm trees. All manner of animals and critters scurried through the plants around them, and fruits grew high in the trees. Young Forrest lost himself in the trees, rapt by the new discoveries, in his eyes at least.

The Santa Maria sat moored in the shallow water, and as he stood on a rocky outcrop, his eyes found Captain Arnaz. The old man scurried over the deck, his attention focused on the water. He never stood still. Something about his movements caught Forrest's attention. He felt a shudder run through him. From his vantage point, he saw a shadow move over the water, like a cloud passing before the sun. Forrest looked into the sky, the cloudless, endless azure. His gaze returned to the water, and the shadow was gone.

"Forrest, Forrest, come down, we need to head back to the boat," Arnold called from the beach. Forrest looked down at his father and waved his acknowledgement.

"Coming, Father." Forrest smiled.

With spirits high, Arnold even allowed Forrest to row the boat a short way back to the *Santa Maria*.

Captain Arnaz met them as they climbed on board. His white face and the distant gaze in his eyes made for an unsettling welcome. He looked at Forrest, his eyes seeming to cut through the lad.

"I need to have a word with you, Mr. Jones," the old captain spoke, and even his voice sounded terrified.

"Evie, why don't you take Forrest down below deck for a bite to eat?" Arnold said to his wife, understanding the imminent conversation was not something his son, or his wife, should be privy to.

Evelyn also understood, and hurried Forrest below deck, where she made him sandwiches with fresh cured ham and slices of cheese.

Above them on the deck, Arnold and Captain Arnaz were locked in deep conversation. The solitude of their location and the fine weather meant that even the most hushed of whispers carried down.

"What are they talking about, Mother?" Forrest asked as he picked up another sandwich.

"I don't know, darling," Evelyn answered.

Without warning, the boat began to rock, swaying back and forth as if riding over a great wave.

The sudden and unexpected motion of the boat brought Forrest up onto the deck. The thrill-seeker in him wanted to be close to the sea swell around them.

Forrest was disappointed. The sea around the boat was calm, almost calmer than at any point in the day. The sky above them still a cloudless, brilliant blue.

"Get below deck, now!" the voice of Captain Arnaz called out as he ran over the deck, lifting the anchor as he hurried to head back into open water.

"Father, what—?" Forrest began.

"You heard the captain, below deck, now!" Arnold shouted, as he began to turn the ship's wheel, following the directions Captain Arnaz bellowed at him.

The frantic nature of his father's voice had Forrest stunned, and for a few moments, he remained standing.

The boat caught the gentle breeze, and as per its design, they soon found themselves moving through the water.

"Get down now, lad. There's nothing here for you to see," Captain Arnaz spoke again. He moved before Forrest, his face sheened in sweat.

"Come on, Forrest, come and help me." Evelyn placed her hands on Forrest's shoulder, turning him around.

The moment Forrest turned his back was the moment Captain Arnaz started screaming.

Forrest felt something warm spurt over the back of his neck. His mother froze, the colour draining from her face with a speed that scared Forrest. He turned, drawn by temptation, but also pushed through the fear of his mother's reaction. His mother made no attempt to stop him. Forrest looked at the captain. He stood in the same place, only a thick brown tentacle now wrapped around his waist. Blood bubbled from his mouth and slicked his beard.

His eyes went wide, and his mouth fell open. A strange suction sound came from his throat. The tentacle around his waist convulsed, as if drinking him. Blood coated the appendage, which stiffened, and with a swift tug pulled away, shearing the captain's body in two. For a brief moment, there was a strip of tentacle thick daylight between the two halves. The slimy, foul-smelling appendage withdrew back into the water, smearing raw meat over the deck.

"Forrest," Arnold called, charging towards his son. "Run."

Forrest felt the rush of air and threw himself to the floor, slipping in the spreading pool of blood. He fell face first to the floor just as a thinner tentacle whipped over his head.

Looking up, Forrest screamed. The tentacle pierced his father's chest, striking hard and fast, withdrawing just as quick.

Arnold fell to his knees, the blood slowly starting to spread over his white shirt. Forrest ran, slipped and skidded his way to his father, who had since fallen to his knees.

"Forrest ... run ..." Arnold wheezed, his hand gripping his son's and squeezing tight.

Forrest stifled a cry of pain from his father's grip. More tentacles appeared, some as thick as a man. They scurried over the deck, tearing splinters into the wooden surface, making the boat rock from side to side, slapping against the water, which crashed up onto the deck.

Evelyn screamed and fled back below the deck. A tentacle shot after her, wrapping around her waist. The limb gave a sharp tug and pulled her out from the stairwell and up into the air. Blood sprayed in every direction as the angry cephalopod limb shook her to death. Her body snapped in two and fell to the deck with a wet smack.

At the same time, another tentacle tugged at Arnold's, now silent figure. His hand was still locked around his son's.

Forrest screamed as he saw the slimy limb wrap around his father's head. Instantly, he heard the sound of flesh and bone being crunched and slurped. The tentacle dragged Arnold's body over to the edge of the boat, Forrest pulled along for the ride. He freed his grip but could not bring himself to let go. A swift tug pulled both father and son overboard. Crashing into the ocean, Forrest found his resolve. The cool water called to him, and he began to swim. He pulled himself through the water and over to the free-floating rowboat.

He pulled himself into the life raft just as the tentacles raked themselves over the boat, stripping away the wood, breaking the vessel apart piece by piece. The mast snapped as a long limb wound its way around the wooden pole, grinding the wood away to nothing. Next came the deck, and the crisp snapping and cracking of splintered. In minutes, the upper level of the *Santa Maria* collapsed inwards on itself.

Four thick tentacles wrapped around the remaining shell of the craft, and in a matter of moments, crushed the hull to driftwood.

The larger shards of the ship were then dragged down beneath the surface of the ocean.

The creature disappeared, seemingly satisfied with its catch.

From the row boat, Forrest sat on the bench, clutching the life vest that had been laying in the bottom of the boat. He couldn't move, his eyes transfixed on the sport where until just a few moments before his family had been enjoying an island boat cruise.

Forrest was covered in blood, both his father's and the captain's. He began to shiver as the life raft bobbed up and down on the ripples created from the boats destruction. He gasped and cried, fearing the creature would come back and snatch him away too.

When nothing came, he pulled out the oars and began to row.

At just age seven, Forrest became a man already. Grabbing the oars, he pulled himself to the shoreline. Leaving the boat in the sand on the beach, he went back to the hotel and contacted the authorities. He never told them what really happened. Instead saying the boat ran into problems and started to take on water. He made a point of saying his parents had given their lives to save him.

With no witnesses, no bodies, and no bodies to be found, nobody asked too many questions.

CHAPTER 3

Bill Klout was the site manager for the Nexco Oil Company's largest platform off the Mexican coast. His platform, the central station in the companies Gulf Coast cluster, gave Bill over one hundred and fifty people to account for. The job came with high pressure, but equally high reward, and Bill loved every second of it.

Bill considered himself a fair man. He read and understood all rules and regulations, and enforced the ones paramount to safety on board. However, he was always willing to overlook certain things if it meant that moral remained high. Happy workers became productive workers.

At five o'clock in the morning, with the sun nothing more than a faint warm glow on the horizon, Platform Six's morning shift found themselves gearing up for an early morning drill. Following the analysis of a test sample, a midnight mail requesting fracking push changed everybody's plans. The protestor boats had been subdued, the ringleaders convinced that no such activity was going to happen on the platform.

He smiled as he drank his coffee. People really did not understand the process. He respected their dedication to the cause, but if they got in his way, and started costing him money, then it was a different story. Reduced returns at the end of the run affected his bonus, and that directly impacted his family. The one thing in the world that Bill would not accept was something interfering with his family.

Somewhere on the rig, an alarm began to sound. Alarms on an oil rig never meant anything good, but Bill trusted his crew, and knew they could handle anything.

Until the phone started ringing.

"We have a problem with pump five," the voice at the other end of the line spoke without waiting for introductions.

"I'll be right down," Bill answered.

He put the phone down, drained the rest of his coffee and left the office. The drilling level was close to the main bridge, but Bill was running by the time he arrived.

"What's going on?" he asked as he reached out to steady himself.

The platform shuddered and shook hard enough for the entire crew to have been brought to the edges of the various levels of the rig. Alarms and sirens were screaming.

"No idea, we were working on the first blast of the morning, and suddenly everything went to hell," Mitch Stevens, the drill chief, answered.

Mitch's eyes widened with fear, well-hidden fear, but nonetheless, Bill did not like the expression on his drill chief's face. Having worked with Mitch for many years, Bill could not recall a time he ever saw the man flustered. They had been through some hair-raising moments with one another, but Bill had never seen such a look in his friend's eyes.

"We need to shut this pump down now. Pull out of the hole," Bill ordered, running through the standard operating protocol.

"We have, and we can't," Mitch answered as he moved nervously from one foot to another.

"What do you mean?" Bill asked, confused.

"We have shut the pump down. That's not what is shaking this place. We can't withdraw, something is holding the drill bit in place," Mitch answered fast, his eyes staring through Bill and out to sea.

"That's not possible," Bill answered.

Behind him, people began to call out and yell. Not the celebratory bellows of an oil strike, nor the panicked yells of an emergency lockdown, but rather the terrified girl-like screams of men being shown their impending death and left with no other option than to wait for the reaper to claim them.

Bill turned around as the first tentacle rose out of the water. Rising above the rig, the slick body was thicker than the legs that held the base tethered in place. On the underside, large suction cups pulsated, as if puckering for a kiss.

"What the hell?" Bill began, but he never finished his exclamation.

The platform gave a groan that rumbled like thunder as the iron frame twisted and bent in a fashion no metal had ever been designed to do. All around him windows began to shatter, raining down razor sharp shards of glass. The sky darkened as more tentacles appeared, wrapping themselves around the structure, squeezing the frame.

Men fell from the balconies above him, landing on the lower levels, their bodies bursting from impact with the metal grating of the base floor. Tiny chunks of blood, bone and gristle then dripped down to the lowest levels. The screams of his crew echoed in Bill's head, but they were ultimately drowned out by the sound of the rig's legs shattering. With a lurch, the platform moved and came free, crashing into the now wild water below them. The ocean rose up and swept many of the men out to sea. Several resisted the pull of the ocean, instead choosing to hold onto their rig, refusing to let the sea claim them.

None of them stood a chance. Smaller tentacles writhed like snakes over the ocean's surface and steadily picked off the bodies that drifted their way.

Bill stood, dumbfounded, paralyzed by fear. The rig tore apart beneath his feet. The solid metal grounding disappeared, revealing a black hole that fell into the ocean, and just beyond that, into the steadily rising beak-like maw of the creature they had awoken.

Bill and many of his co-workers hit the water just as the monstrous beak emerged from the waves. Their impact on its second set of jaws broke their bodies and split them open, spilling their warm innards into the sea. Tasting blood, the secondary mouth opened and sucked everything down deep into the belly of the beast.

Explosions and fires ripped through what remained of the rig, and oil began to pump into the ocean from the severed lines that ran beneath the surface.

Within minutes, the beast tore the rig apart. The monster did not spare a single living soul, and vanished into the oceans just as quickly as it had risen.

CHAPTER 4

Off the coast of Florida, July 30th, 2016

The *August Sunrise* was a busy fishing boat. One of the more popular ones for deep water fishing. A thirty-eight foot Blackwater 38SFX with a five-hundred-gallon fuel capacity, fifteen hundred horsepower outboard engines and a basic weight of twelve-thousand five-hundred pounds, she possessed all the requirements you would need to be a successful fishing craft. Sleek, sexy and strong as an ox.

Frank Jeffries and his sons, Iain and Rory, had hired her for a three-day expedition. Three different fishing grounds, ready to catch some of the biggest fish in the sea.

The first day went well, with each of the three catching a mix of snappers and sailfish. The second day brought the real excitement in the form of a big old swordfish. They did not win the battle, but the stories they were able to tell about the fight that ensued meant they all had one heck of a good time. The weather deteriorated and resulted in the day being cut the day short just as they caught wind of some tuna fish.

The storm that rolled in was a beast, lasting all afternoon and into the evening. Winds and rain unlike anything they had seen before. The storm came from nothing and built up into a frenzy before falling down and disappearing twice as fast.

The resort had suffered some damage, and several people sustained injuries when pool chairs and palm trees were sent blustering along their path, but come morning, the sun was shining, the forecasts looked perfect, and the Jeffries boys could not wait to get back out and catch whatever they could on their final day.

"We've got reports of some quality-sized tuna fish a little further out than the last two days. The day will be a little longer, but should make up for the shorter trip yesterday." Captain Pete told them as he pulled the boat out of the harbour and toward the open sea.

"Thanks, that sounds like a great time to me," Frank said as he and his boys exchanged high-fives.

The trip out took them a few hours. They were not alone, however; plenty of other boats shared the same idea. Captain Pete pointed out that the storm agitated the fish, gotten them ready to bite; always a good line to sell the tourists.

"We're not stopping here though. I came out early this morning and picked up something on the sonar. A big old shadow ripe for the picking," Captain Pete said with a laugh. "You men are in for a treat."

They left the bulk of the pleasure cruisers and smaller fishing companies behind, heading deeper into the open water.

"Those are some beauties." Rory pointed to the horizon where some even larger vessels were hard at work dragging their lines and setting up for the day.

"Yep, we are at the boundary of the professional waters. Recent regulations put a boundary line in for pleasure boats like this one, and the real pros. I don't mind none, but sometimes you have to the push the boundaries just a little." Captain Pete opened a beer and took a long drink.

Not long later, they shut off the motor and got the lines ready. One of each side and one from the stern. Each of the Jeffries clan would have a chance behind the big reel, as had been their agreement all week. As always, Frank claimed seniority and took the first round.

"The sonar had them coming this way. I would expect them to be passing us by soon enough," Pete said as he climbed back up to the deck from the cabin. He had a cooler in his arm, which he placed on the floor of the boat. "I brought something for you all to enjoy. Help yourself."

Thirty minutes later, the boat was still, the men each with a line cast and a smile on their faces. Within minutes, Rory's line began to spin. "I've got something here," he called out as he struggled to control the line.

"Reel that bugger in, boy," Frank exclaimed with delight.

"I'm trying, but fuck me this bastard is a beast," Rory grunted, sweat already dripping from his brow. He held the rod with a white-knuckled grip.

"I've got something too," Iain called out and his line began to speed away from them.

"Holy hell, me too. We've got a damned trifecta, boys," Frank cried out, his joy bordering on delirium.

Behind them, they heard Captain Pete come running. None of the men paid him much attention, for they were too busy trying not to lose both the rod and themselves overboard.

"Cut the motherfucking lines!" Pete yelled as he ran from brother to brother, and finally to son.

"What, are you crazy?" Frank snarled.

Pete gave a cry as none of the men listened to him. He turned and ran up to the wheelhouse, just as the boat began to lurch in the water. He gunned the engines, maxed out the throttle and put all fifteen-hundred horsepower into pulling against the force that tugged at his boat.

Pete didn't look back. He held no inclination to get a second look. Instead, his eyes studied the horizon, and for the first time in many years, Pete Colden prayed. He heard his boat groan and begin to break apart. The first rod tore away from its fixture and crashed over the deck and into the ocean. A few moments later, the second suffered the same fate, splintering the *August Sunrise's* siding.

Pete heard the shouts of his customers, their protestations, but he ignored them. He cursed at his boat and slapped the wheel in an attempt to generate extra speed. With two of the rods gone, all of the pressure transitioned over to the third rod. The main heavy-duty line tore free and crashed through the end board, smashing a hole almost down to the waterline. The *August* was free and jumped out of the water as its power was redirected into free forward movement.

Pulling the brakes, bringing his boat to a neutral sputter, Pete turned to face the three men. "I said to cut the damned lines." His breaths came hard and laboured, as if he had just out-sprinted the devil himself.

"What the hell is wrong with you?" Frank started shouting, only to stop when Iain laid a hand on his shoulder.

"Dad, look," he called, pointing out to see. They could see four other boats, each one in varying stages of destruction. Large brown tentacles shot out of the water and grabbed at the boats. They wrapped around them and effortlessly crushed them, dragging them beneath the waves in a flurry of activity. The sea frothed and foamed and within a matter of seconds

"What the hell was that?" Rory asked, turning towards Pete, as if he had the answers they needed.

"Damned if I know. I won't see my boat eaten by some sea monster." He turned and pushed the throttle once more. "Hold on tight."

The *August Sunrise* sped home but limped into port. The damage to the frame and the stress on the engines meant that the craft's days were numbered.

News travelled fast, and by the time they pulled into the harbour, a decent-sized crowd stood waiting for them, eager to speak to the men who escaped the sea monster's death-dealing clutches.

The three tourists, buoyed by the cooler of beer, were more than happy to talk about their escape from the jaws of death. Until the alcohol on their breath and the slur in their words destroyed the trace of credibility their story held.

Pete slipped away into the crowd; he held no desire to be a face in the papers, or to become the crazy old man who told stories of sea monsters in order to lure people to hire him for day's fishing and adventure.

Instead, Pete moved back to his apartment. He closed and locked the door, before picking up the phone and dialling the number he had for an old friend.

CHAPTER 5

Stories of fishermen and sea monsters were common place, but never failed to get the news teams salivating. The tale of the Jeffries boys held great premise; however, their clear inebriation saw the mood sink. The credibility of their story dropped and everybody turned and left. Only one man remained in the harbour, watching the three men. An older man, with a shock of white hair and a once white beard, now stained yellow that stretched down to his chest and out in all directions.

"What do you want, old man?" Frank Jeffries growled, his anger at people refusing to believe their story manifesting behind a temper.

The man said nothing for a while, but observed the three men with his piercing green eyes. He was old, just not as old as he looked. His body looked small and fragile, yet his eyes shone with a youth and vitality that Rory found unsettling.

"Just leave him be, Dad. Let's go back to the hotel. I've got work again the day after tomorrow." Rory tried to pull his father away but the confrontation was set.

"I asked you a question, asshole," Frank snapped.

"I know you did, and I am trying to decide if you are worth my time answering or not," the old man answered with a snarl of his own.

The response floored Frank, who did not know how to respond. Not normally an angry man, confrontation was not natural ground from him to base a conversation in.

"I know what happened out there. I know what that creature is," the man spoke again, seeming to understand that the anger in the early exchange was not indicative of either man's natural character.

"You do?" Iain answered for his father.

"Yes."

"What was it?" Rory stuttered. "No way a single creature did all that. It took out four boats and almost us too. I mean for something to do that … the creature must be enormous to … to…"

"I haven't seen the creature for many years, I was just a kid, but I guarantee you one thing. That creature is real. That thing killed my family, and I've been hunting it ever since. I guess the storm yesterday woke the fucker up, and now she's hungry." The old man moved from his position above the men and down to the dock level. "The name is Forrest, and what you gentlemen met on the water, was the Kraken."

The three Jeffries men looked at each other and slowly began to laugh. A nervous, snorted kind of laugh, one made of equal parts absurdity and fear.

"You can laugh, but you know I am telling the truth. That beast is awake and if what you say is true, she has grown. Nobody is safe. Nobody." Forrest glared at the men, and the fire in his eyes held them all still.

"I don't know what that thing was, so you can use any name you want, mister. All I know is I saw a monster. We are leaving tomorrow, and as far as I am concerned, that's the end of the matter," Frank said, a tremor in his voice. "I'm a semi-retired insurance broker from Pennsylvania, I'm not interested in hunting sea monsters, or having anything to do with them in any way, shape, or form."

"I understand that, but let me buy you men a drink, you met the Kraken and lived. That's more than anybody else I know can say." Forrest smiled, his teeth yellowed through age.

The three men followed him to the bar. The moment they entered, the place fell silent. Just like in the old westerns when a stranger walks into a saloon. Everybody stopped what they were doing to stare at the new group. The whispers began as they walked through the bar, over to a table in the corner.

The old man sat down and motioned for the others to do the same. He fished out a pack of cigarettes, lit one and took a drag so deep he burned away half of the stick in one take.

"Usual, Forrest?" the middle-aged barmaid asked as she came up to the table.

"Please, Lauren." Forrest winked at her. "The same for my friends here."

"Sure thing," she answered, smiling and turning around almost before she had arrived.

"That's service," Frank said, trying to joke.

"People like to keep me out of the way," Forrest answered with a serious tone.

"Why is that?" Rory asked.

"Because Forrest here is crazy as a loon, spouting nonsense about sea monsters and creatures that killed his family," a large drunk man slurred as he staggered up to the table. "You fellas ought to let this nonsense drop. Hanging around with him ain't going to do you no good."

"Fuck you, Wilbur," Forrest snarled, his eyes flaring as he stared at the drunk.

"Wilbur, that's enough." The barmaid had returned and pushed the drunk man away from the table.

An attractive woman, in a plain, everyday sense of the word, from the minimal makeup plastered against her face to her shoulder-length brunette hair, pulled back in a simple ponytail. Her hips were a little wide, her body a little larger than some people would want, but she could still make heads turn. Not that anybody would (dare) call Lauren fat. With an ample bosom and great-looking legs, almost everybody would have considered themselves luck to end the night with Lauren squeezing them in a straddle. Her hazel eyes and freckles gave her a cheeky, youthful look that added to her charm, and for something a little extra, her foul mouth was able to make even the most hardened seamen blush. Swearing never sounded as hot as when spat from Lauren's lips.

"I didn't mean nothing, Lauren, you know that," Wilbur protested as he turned and walked away.

"Sorry about that, gents. Wilbur is an asshole when he's drunk … when he's sober too." She laughed and handed out their drinks. "If you did see anything today, then Forrest here is the man to talk to. He knows everything about the creatures that live out in the water."

***

Captain Randolph Wiseman was still asleep when the phone started ringing. He had been up all night helping his daughter mend a nasty leak in her house. Having fallen into bed at eight thirty, the sound of the ringing phone became an instant irritation. He opened his eyes and glared at the clock, the time only served to sharpen the edge of his good humour. Grumbling, he rolled over grabbed his mobile.

"Captain Wiseman, you'd better have a good reason for waking me up, asshole," he grumbled the usual early morning greeting.

"Randy, it's Pete Colden." The introduction was enough to clear the fog from Randolph's mind.

"Pete, Jesus Christ, it's been years. I thought you were dead." Randolph sat upright in bed and swung his feet over the edge and into the slippers that sat waiting for him.

"I don't have time to explain, but I need to meet. I ... there is something out in water ... dammit, she's back, Randy. She's awake," Pete said.

For Randolph Wiseman, the world stopped. Time stood still, and for a brief moment, everything ceased to exist. A swarming darkness settled over him, and for a moment, the idea of giving himself over to it held a certain attraction.

"How can you be so sure?" he asked.

"I was out on the water. I've seen her with my own eyes. She's grown too." Randolph dressed while Pete continued his explanation. He got off the phone, kissed his wife on the cheek, and stole a piece her toast before disappearing out of the door.

Abigail Wiseman had been married to a military man her whole life. She no longer questioned anything that happened at such a rush. She recognized the look on her husband's face, having seen the same expression often enough over the years to know that he would not tell her anyway. She didn't mind, because when things were that bad, she did not want to know.

Pete hung up the phone and sat back in his living room. A cold sweat coated his body, and he could not stop his hands from shaking. He kept telling himself he had imagined it all. He refused to believe the creature could have returned, after all those years, but yet, he had seen her with his own eyes. He found a degree of comfort in the knowledge that Randolph agreed to come help, but alone, he doubted the two of them would be able to accomplish much.

Grabbing himself a drink, Pete sat back in his favourite armchair and waited.

***

Forrest left his new friends in a drunken stupor at the bar. None of them were sober enough to remember the exact moment when he left.

Forrest left the bar with all of the information he needed to know. They happily gave him the rough coordinates of where the monster had been, and the name of the man who had taken them out fishing. Forrest and Pete Colden were no strangers to one another. Both heavy drinkers, the only real difference between them being that Forrest could control his alcohol intake. Yet, while their paths had crossed over the years, neither man would describe the other as anything more than an acquaintance.

Still, Forrest found himself standing on Pete's doorstep not forty minutes later, his fist hammering on the door.

"What do you want?" Pete asked, talking through the chained door.

"I think we need to talk," Forrest said as he glared at the man.

"I don't think so." Pete moved to close the door, but Forrest pushed his foot between the door and the frame, preventing Peter from escaping.

"You know what I am talking about, and you know I know you do, so now is time for full disclosure. No secrets. You to tell me what you know, and I will tell you what I have found out over the years." Forrest was not in the mood to play games.

Pete froze. His eyes locked on the old man. Everybody in town knew all about Forrest Jones and his crazy stories. Most called him harmless, several called him crazy. Pete would have called him dangerous.

With a sigh, Pete nodded his head, closed the door and took off the chain.

"Come in, we have a lot to talk about," Pete muttered.

The two men sat in silence for a while, Pete nursing a beer, while Forrest smoked his third cigarette since arriving. They sat opposite each other watching, neither willing make the first move.

"The creature killed my parents back in fifty-two," Forrest finally spoke.

"I first saw her when I was in the Navy back in the early eighties," Pete offered in return.

The silence returned.

"We need to call somebody," Forrest said.

"Already did," Pete answered.

Their staccato back and forth continued for a while until suddenly, without either of them noticing, something changed. The two men started talking like friends. Their stories were no longer single statements, but long, flowing narratives. They swapped stories and tales. Forrest was true to his word. He explained everything he had learned over the years, not skipping a single detail.

"'I've been tracking this creature for over sixty years. I've roamed the country, the world, following sightings and rumours. I came close, but only once did I get real close, back in the summer of seventy-nine. Off the coast of Ireland of all places. Something wiped out an entire fishing fleet during a storm. They just disappeared without a trace. People blamed the storm, and I don't blame them for it. I ain't seen a storm like that since. Lightning as bright as daylight and thunder that rolled in your ears like jet engines up close. A few people claimed to have seen something, but they put it down to the tricks of the sea. Who wants to become the old fool blabbering on about sea monsters?" Forrest sat back and opened his beer.

"We came across her for the first time back in eighty-three, not far from here, off the coast of Mexico. I was in the Navy back then and we blasted her out of the water. We must have killed the thing, nothing could take those shots and keep living, but when we went to check, we couldn't find the body anywhere. I still don't see how it could have survived. For the next four years, we stood back and waited. Nobody reported any fresh sightings, and eventually the task force got disbanded. We all got relocated given our pick of locations too. So I headed down to the Keys, and took a simple desk job for the last few years. Retired back in nineteen-ninety. I never even thought about that beast again until you came to town," Pete said as he raised his beer bottle and drank deeply.

"I can't believe that she has just been sitting out there ever since. I mean, for what?" Forrest asked.

"I don't know. My guess is some sort of hibernation or some other shit like that. All I know is that some big ass creature is out in that ocean. I don't know if it is our monster or not, but the fucker is enormous. Anyway, a buddy of mine is heading down on a flight right now. We served together back then. He is still in the Navy today. If this thing pans out, we will bring the fight to this bitch, and this time, she ain't getting away from us. Are you in?" Pete looked at Forrest, his eyes stone-cold sober, in spite of the litany of bottles at his feet.

"Hell yes. This thing needs to pay for killing my family." Forrest drained his beer and slammed the bottle down onto the table top.

"Great. Meet us here tomorrow morning, early. I want to head out onto the water and see what we can find."

CHAPTER 6

Forrest did not return home after leaving Pete behind to the rest of his beers. Instead, he headed to the harbour and boarded his own small craft. With his berth being on the opposite side to the *August Sunrise*, Forrest could not inspect the damage to Pete's boat, but he did not need to. He had first-hand knowledge of what the beast could do, and to much larger vessels.

Climbing into his own Grady-White Freedom 250, Forrest powered up the engine and headed out to sea. He held no intentions of tackling the creature, but his mind was restless, his recent dreams plagued by the memories of his family and that fateful day off the Cuban coast. For the last week, he woke every night, screaming and wracked with panic. Even the drink, the one device that had gotten him through the worst of times, failed to dull the pain.

Taking his boat, Forrest sped away from the coast, enjoyed the freedom of having the wind in his air, the salty smell of the ocean in his nose and the great open expanse all around him. Forrest still remembered the advice given to him by Captain Arnaz all of those years ago. Respect the ocean. She was his mistress, and he was but a slave to her call. He enjoyed her company, and could not imagine living life any other way.

During the years, Forrest had made several upgrades to the boats applications. He had installed a state-of-the-art deep water sonar at quite some expense. Sitting with his engine idle, five miles off the coast, the sun rapidly setting behind him, he turned up the machine eager to see what he could find. He picked up several blips, small schools of fish and possible a few rogue sharks looking for an evening meal.

Forrest finally began to relax. He studied the sonar when suddenly something large shot across the screen. The long, thin mass shot through one of the large blips that Forrest had taken to be a school of Mahi-Mahi.

A moment later and the erroneous blip was gone, along with the school of … whatever.

Forrest jumped to his feet. The light was fading rapidly, but he could make out the water's surface. The ocean was alive, the surface bubbling as if boiling. Fish thrashed and crashed against one another as their frantic attempts to escape the water amounted to nothing.

The tentacles shot through the bubbling mass of fish, cutting through the creatures, staining the churning surface red. The stench of fish guts wafted on the wind. Further out to sea, Forrest saw something that made his blood freeze in his veins. An enormous brown mass rose above the surface, indistinguishable at such a great distance. Two long, thin tentacles with flattened edges whistled over the sea, crashing down and scooping the mass of scared fish towards the hungry beak.

Forrest jumped behind the wheel of his boat, the *Melville* and redlined the engines all the way back to the shore. He took the boat to the harbour, tied everything off and hurried home as fast as his aged legs could carry him.

Forrest found Pete's number online by searching for his fishing tour company. Dialling with trembling fingers, he paced the living area of his small home restlessly, like a polar bear in the zoo.

Pete answered on the third straight time of ringing.

"Who is this?" he growled, clearly not used to receiving calls so late in the day.

"It's Forrest. I need you to grab your friend and meet me at my place. No questions, no arguments. Just collect him and bring your asses over here, ASAP." Forrest gave the address and hung up, not giving Pete a second to question his actions.

Forrest was still pacing his room when his two guests arrived. He heard their car pull up, and opened the door as they walked up.

"Come in, come in," he said panicked.

First impressions count for a lot, and for Randolph Wiseman, his first introduction to Forrest Jones seemed to prove he conformed to every crazy hermit stereotype ever used.

Forrest hurried the two men inside, and the one look at the state of the house did nothing to convince Randolph that he had made the right decision in listening to his old friend. Randolph understood why his old friend chose to wander down an alcohol-lined path, but it remained a weakness, and weakness lead to, among other things, unreliability. Standing in a house filled from floor to ceiling with boxes and loose papers with a near manic, wild-looking man rushing around, rummaging through the piles, Randolph asked himself if he had made a terrible mistake in answering his friend's call.

"What is going on here?" Randolph asked, raising his voice not to a shout, but to a level that demanded attention.

Pete turned to look at his friend, an apology building, but Forrest beat him to the punch.

"I'm sorry. I must look half-mad. If you give me a moment, I can explain everything. You see, well, I was out on the water tonight and I saw it. I saw the creature, and she is enormous. I just cannot get the image out of my head," Forrest blurted, the words spilling faster and faster, the excitement coming through in his voice.

"Slow down, slow down. What are you talking about?" Randolph asked.

"You know what I'm talking about. The Kraken. She's here, something woke her up and she is mad as hell." Randolph's green eyes burned behind his bushy eyebrows and thick beard.

Randolph waited a moment and smiled. "Just checking."

"Clever man, clever man." Forrest nodded. "Anyway, this is everything I could dredge up in over sixty years of tracking this beast. Everything from sightings, to police reports and fishing charts. Coast Guard information and even a few Navy documents. Then through here, you will find boxes and boxes of myths, legends, stories, movies and newspaper clippings."

"Wow, you certainly are thorough," Pete said, looking around at the unstable piles and pillars. Pages yellowed with age, curled and broken.

"You got pretty close too, looking at all of this," Randolph spoke, clearly impressed as he leafed through a randomly plucked paper file from the desk.

"You don't know the half of it," Forrest said as he walked back into the living room with a fresh stack of papers.

"What is that?" Randolph asked, his attention fully caught.

"I believe this is the alarm clock that woke up our monster. Take a look." Forrest walked over to the men, his small frame hunched over from years of sitting bent over books and desks, scouring every scrap of paper for information.

"Nexco Oil," Pete read the name aloud. "I've heard of them. They were in the news recently." The drunken slur gone from his words.

"They operate one of the largest oil rig clusters in the Mexican Gulf. All over the world really. But just a few days ago, something happened. During a fracking drill out on their main rig, something went wrong, because that rig isn't there anymore." Forrest turned the page in his print out and showed the others.

"You mean the rig found something and moved to a new location?" Pete asked, still turning the pages.

"No, I mean the fucking rig is gone, vanished from the middle of the ocean. More than one-hundred and fifty crew members too," Forrest corrected the man.

"You think that their fracking campaign released the Kraken?" Randolph looked from the paperwork to Forrest and back again, several times.

"I'm just putting the pieces together. That's all I have ever been doing." Forrest moved and sat in the old wooden chair behind his desk, which creaked as he sat. Much like the man using it; however, the passage of time had not yet rendered either useless.

"I think you could be onto something, but ultimately this is just nice to know. If that beast is back, and truly as large as you say, then all that matters is bringing an end to its existence. I mean permanently this time." The authoritative air in Randolph's voice rose up. He was a man of action, a man used to making decisions.

"Will you make the call?" Pete said, looking over to his old friend.

"That is not going to be very easy. Admiral Belgrave retired two years ago, and died last August. I don't know how we are going to convince them of anything unless we deliver some real proof." Randolph stalled. He left home, fully expecting this moment would come. He did not travel across the country simple to see an old friend and talk war stories. "I'll make the call."

"I'll make the coffee," Forrest said and offered his hand out to the old Navy captain.

Randolph offered his own and was not surprised by the strength behind the old man's grip.

"How do you drink yours?" Forrest asked.

"As black as my soul," Randolph answered.

CHAPTER 7

Felix Anderson was a deck hand on board the *Santa Fe*, one of three boats in a small private fleet. He had only been working on the boat for two seasons, and while the work was hard, both the literal and figurative meanings of the word, he thoroughly enjoyed what he did for a living. He was not a man unafraid of the grind, and always ensured that he worked harder than anybody else. He did not do it with malice in his motives, he just could not fight the way he had been raised. Work hard, play hard. His mother had drummed that way of thinking into him, even more so after his elder brother fell in with the local gangs, a move that would later cost him his life. Felix's work rate and ethic did not go unnoticed. The men in charge of the small fishing company held him in high regard. Felix just hoped that if he kept working hard, he would one day be in-line for a promotion.

Felix ignored the thick brown lump floating on the surface of the water, but once he realized that it was not just debris but seemed to be following their boat, he started to feel uneasy. Leaning over the side, he stared at the lump which was as wide as a tree and much larger than first impressions made believe. Both ends disappeared below the surface of the water, looping back on themselves.

The *Santa Fe's* hull brushed against the lump, which jerked in response, as if snatched from slumber. The water rippled suddenly, the thing vanished.

Felix shivered as he looked around to see if the others also noticed anything strange. If they had, nobody gave any sign of alarm.

A few moments later, the boat began to rock. Something tapped against the hull, a steady tap-tap-tap, like someone tapping a wall to find the right spot to drill.

There was no doubt that everybody heard the noise. They all froze.

"What is that?" a large, stocky man by the name of Barnes asked.

"It's nothing," the captain of the vessel answered. Steve Finch was a relaxed man. He treated his crew well, and everybody enjoyed working under his command.

"Let's all get back to business. I want to head home early today," he said as he turned back to the main equipment console. "What the hell?"

He never got to finish the statement because his chest exploded, sending chunks of meat and lung tissue spurting over the equipment. He looked down and found a squirming brown worm-like creature protruding from his chest. The foreign object extended at least a foot from his body, the tip a rounded point. He curled upwards, as if somehow able to see the man, before clamping down on his flesh.

From the deck, the crew were helpless to do anything but stand and stare as their captain was torn in half. Thick purple strands of intestines tumbled from his severed upper portion, pouring over the deck like spilled chum.

More of the tentacles appeared around the boat, rising up to create a cage of stinking sea-flesh. The stench of rot was overpowering as the tentacles rose up and around the craft. Smaller tentacles snaked over the deck, slurping up the spilled innards, sucking them through the suction cups on the underside of their bulk. Others found the crew. They wrapped around their ankles, shot up their trouser legs, tearing through flesh, driven further by the scent of fresh blood.

One by one, the crew was broken down and stripped away until nothing remained but a deck filled with spilled organs swimming in blood, and Felix. Felix stood unharmed on the deck as all around him carnage was wrought. When finished, the tentacles slipped back down beneath the water's surface.

Terrified, Felix didn't dare move, and that was how they found him. The following day, after the boat had been reported missing by the others in the small fleet, the Coast Guard sprang into action. A search and rescue attempt launched at the crack of dawn. They located the boat without issue, bobbing on the ocean current not too far off the projected course.

Jenna Harrington, the lieutenant in charge of the *USCGC Stratton,* led by example, setting foot on the *Santa Fe* before the rest of her crew. This made her the first target to be jumped by a frantic Felix Anderson. He clung to her, his body stiffened by fear, his grip as tight as an anaconda's.

"Lieutenant," the cry went up.

"Stand down, stand down," Jenna called out, pushing Felix away from her.

Behind her, the three-man crew all stood with their M16's raised and ready to use if the need arose.

"What the heck happened here?" Jenna addressed the terrified young man. He was caked in dried blood and the only noises he made were a babbled gargle.

"Jesus wept, look at this place," Ensign Luke Watson said as his eyes swept the *Santa Fe.*

"I am only going to ask you this one more time. What happened?" Jenna elected to draw her 9mm M9. She pointed her weapon at the man, but even that seemed to serve as no great motivator for him to start talking.

All that came from her threat was an added pool of dark yellow urine, which leaked down Felix's leg to mingle with the now rust-coloured, blood-stained deck.

"Oh for the love of God," Jenna snarled. A sweet yet battle hardened woman, she had seen things and done things that many others of her age and gender could never understand. The life she chose made her more than a little blunt in her mannerisms. "Take this guy out of here. Lock him up until we can determine what happened and how he is involved."

The still babbling Felix was escorted off the *Santa Fe,* handcuffed and led to a holding cell on the *Stratton.* Only Jenna and her second-in-command Junior Lieutenant James Winslow remained on the stricken fishing vessel.

"Where are the bodies?" James asked, trying to keep his voice steady.

"I have no idea. Looking at the blood and … bits left over, I would say we are down at least three men, if not more," Jenna answered moving around the boat, her M9 still held at the ready.

The deck of the *Santa Fe* was open and the craft offered no real room for anybody to hide. Together, the pair searched the lower level, including the storage tank.

"There's nobody else," Jenna remarked as she pushed the door to the strange bay closed. "One thing is for sure. The captain didn't know what the hell he was doing. This boat is a fucking health hazard. There is no way he was operating according to fishing regulations."

"The ship isn't in great condition either. She's a new boat, but doesn't have a long life ahead of her I can tell you that." James nodded.

"Longer than its crew," Jenna said coldly.

On board the *Stratton*, Felix was taken straight to the holding cells on the second deck, and thrown into a holding cell. A guard stood outside the locked door, but Felix made no attempt to resist. He went where guided, and sat on the bed in the room. If anything, he seemed more relieved to be locked up than anything.

"Has he said anything yet?" Jenna asked as she walked down the corridor.

"No, Lieutenant. He is just sitting there," Ensign Francis Laporte answered.

"I'll take it from here. You go get something to eat and come back," Jenna said, relieving the young man from his duties.

Once alone, Jenna unlocked the door and entered the cell. Felix flinched at the groan the opening door gave, but for the rest, he remained as distant as ever.

Jenna moved beside him and sat down. She said nothing. The ship rocked on the ocean. Jenna always found it to be a calming motion.

The minutes ticked by and Jenna simply sat with the man. His shivering stopped, his breathing became steady, taking on the same rhythm as the rolling waves.

"You will think I am crazy," he spoke in a broken voice. His lips were dry, this throat cracked.

"I promise you that I will not judge you," Jenna spoke beside him. "I think you witnessed something terrible. I don't believe you killed everybody on that boat. So tell me what happened and we can fix this. You are safe with us."

"Nobody is safe from that thing," the man spoke and promptly began to shake once more.

"What thing?" Jenna caught wind of the word and wanted to know more.

"It … it was a sea monster." The man paused, waiting for the laughter to come. "It came from under us. It killed the captain, tore him up. The others too. We never stood a chance."

"A sea monster?" Jenna tried hard to keep her tone serious but even the hard-edge lieutenant struggled to keep a proper tone.

"There were tentacles and things. They came out of the water and …" His voice trailed off.

"You mean an octopus?" Jenna asked, trying to relate the man's description to something based in the real world.

"Of sorts. But bigger. Much bigger. It ripped a man apart. Its arms were as thick as tree trunks, carried on under the water. It was a monster, I'm telling you the truth." Felix spoke faster and faster.

"OK, OK, I believe you. You are safe now, safe here with us. What's your name?" Jenna asked.

"Felix, you can call me Felix," he answered.

"Very well. I believe you, Felix, but I will need you to stay down here a little moment longer. Can you do that?" Jenna had a bad feeling growing in the pit of her stomach, and had no clue how to shift it.

"OK, I will wait here. Just make sure that if you see this creature, you run." Felix looked at Jenna as he spoke. While the desperation in his voice was worrying, it was the look of sheer terror in his eyes that put her the most on edge.

Jenna left the man and closed the door. She locked it but told the guard that if the prisoner showed no signs of being a danger to himself, he could stand down.

Moving from the lower second deck up to the 01 Deck where she passed her CO office and instead knocked on the door of the XO's Stateroom. James Winslow opened the door and greeted his CO.

"Has he said anything?" he asked.

"Yes, but I don't know what to make of it," Jenna said with a sigh. "I know he didn't kill those people. I just know it, but what he said … it just doesn't make any sense."

***

A short time later, Jenna sat in the XO's office, drinking coffee. The cramped and crowded space familiar to her, having long ago grown accustomed to her XO's filing system. Not that she would have called it a system, but she could not deny that James never failed to locate something in the stacks of paperwork, normally at the first time of asking.

"A sea monster?" James said again, repeating the word for the fourth time, without using anything other than a long, thoughtful pause in between.

"That's what he says. A large octopus-like sea monster killed everybody on board." Jenna nodded.

"But it left him alive?"

"It would seem so," Jenna said her nod continuing. "I know it sounds crazy, but you should hear him talk. It's just so … so convincing."

"With all due respect, Lieutenant, you are not buying this sea monster story, are you?" James asked, incredulous.

"No, I'm not saying that, but …" At that moment, the telephone began to ring. Someone was calling down to them from the bridge.

"Lieutenant, I think you will want to come up and see this," the voice of Richard Green, the sonar technician, spoke.

It was not a statement he needed to make twice. Both Jenna and James stood up and left the room almost immediately.

The bridge was located on 03 Deck, the uppermost level of the cutter class ship. Jenna and James sprinted up the two decks, and reached the bridge in no time. Both felt an uneasy sense of restlessness growing in their stomachs.

They were met by Richard Green, and Chief Petty Officer Bruce 'Bulldog' Brown. A giant of a man and as strong as an ox, Bulldog was pretty much everybody's favourite person on board the ship and in the sector as a whole.

"What have we got, Bulldog?" Jenna asked, striding into the bridge. The waters around them were calm, and that only served to put her even more on edge.

"We have something on radar, ma'am," Richard said, his face a little pale.

"I'm going to need a little more than that," Jenna said, trying to keep her cool.

"Well, we don't know what it is, ma'am. It came and went in an instant, but it was big," Richard continued, growing nervous under the acidic gaze of his CO.

"How big is big?" Jenna demanded.

Richard swallowed hard. "Aircraft carrier big." He watched his CO's face.

"That is big. Well, what the hell was it?" Jenna asked, her patience wearing thin. "I don't see anything, and I cannot believe something as large as an aircraft carrier could just disappear into thin air."

"It … it was under the water, ma'am." Richard lowered his gaze. He had only been on board the *Stratton* for two weeks, and did not want to write his name into his commanding officer's bad books.

"It was organic." Bulldog stepped forward and took over the communication. "It moved like lightning, heading to the north."

"Organic? Is it friendly?" Jenna asked, her gut beginning to churn around the ball that was lodged there.

"We don't—" Bulldog began, when something crashed against the boat.

The impact occurred below the waterline, but the power in it still managed to send everybody in the bridge sprawling. Richard cried out as his leg got caught beneath him, his leg breaking with a crisp, audible snap.

"I need reports. What's going on?" Jenna called into the communication system.

The feedback began to filter through, superficial structure damage, but numerous injuries below deck.

"I want the Bofors online now, get the CIWS also running," Jenna ordered, flipping between the channels without thinking.

"How's his leg?" she asked turning to look at Bulldog. He was crouched down beside the young sonarman.

"It's a clean break. Hurt's like a bitch, but nothing life threatening," Bulldog reported as he rose to his feet. "Brace for contact."

His warning came just in time. Everybody on the bridge managed to brace themselves for the impact. This came from the opposite side and pushed the plus four-hundred-foot long vessel through the water as if it were nothing.

"I need visuals," Jenna called as she spun around, her eyes watching the ocean. "Are the weapons online?"

"Yes, sir, weapons systems are online and ready to rock," the answer came back on the waves of a groggy voice.

"I have sonar contact. It's closing in on us," Bulldog called from behind the sonar station. "It's already under us, partly."

"Get us moving. Full power, I want some room so we can blow this son of a bitch out of the water," Jenna roared.

"Sir, look," the petrified voice of the injured Richard cried out. His eyes went wide with terror and locked on the ocean.

"Jesus help us," Bulldog said, making the sign of the cross over his chest.

Jenna turned around, and her orders fell silent in her throat. The large tentacle rose out of the water and towered above the craft. Almost as wide as the boat, it blocked out the horizon. The large, round suction cups pulsed as if struggling to breath being out of the water.

"I want the guns blazing, now!" Jenna found her voice. "Get this boat moving! Move and fire." She ran from the bridge and down to the 02 Deck where the smaller .50 calibre machine guns were mounted. Swivelling, she opened fire and sent a volley of hot lead into the giant appendage.

The rounds hit the large limb but appeared to do minimal damage. Black blood began to ooze from the wounds, but they closed themselves almost as soon as they began to leak.

Jenna gritted her teeth and sent a long, sustained burst of fire into the tentacle, and was please when Bulldog appeared and got behind the second gun.

With a concentrated burst of gunfire, they managed to open up a gaping wound in the tentacle, which turned from brown to blue colouration and slipped back beneath the waves. A cloud of oily black blood left behind.

"This isn't over, you know that, right?" Bulldog said as they stood staring at the spreading dark cloud.

"Yeah, I know, but it's a victory for now," Jenna said as the boat began to move.

The boat growled as the craft was pushed along at thirty knots, the maximum it could realistically achieve.

"Ma'am, we have multiple targets inbound," Richard grunted.

The rookie impressed Jenna. Even with a compound fracture in his leg, he managed to haul himself behind the sonar console and get back to work. He looked green and was sweating profusely as he tried to ignore the pain. Jenna promised herself she would see it to the young man was rewarded for his actions. Even if he did keep failing to adapt to addressing her correctly.

"How many?" she asked moving to the bridge's main windows.

"I count eight, they are all around us." The panic in his voice clear for them all to hear.

"I want everybody ready to take these motherfuckers down." Jenna still had no real idea what they were up against. "Somebody bring me Felix."

"Who?"

"Felix … the prisoner." She turned to James, who looked just as ashen as Richard.

"Ma'am … sir … Ma'am, they're gone," Richard called, stuttering his words, his head and mouth running at different speeds and in different directions.

"What do you mean gone?" Jenna asked, striding over to the sonar console.

"I mean gone. They just vanished." He stared at the screen.

"You mean they pulled back?" Jenna tried to correct the man.

"No, ma'am. I mean they vanished. It's like they don't exist anymore."

Silence fell over the boat, even the water seemed unnaturally still.

"It changed its body temperature," Bulldog called, just as all hell broke loose.

Eight tentacles shot from the water. Smaller than the large one Jenna and Bulldog had ripped into. They surrounded the boat, whipping around like the snakes on the head of a hydra.

"I want all hands on deck. Locked and loaded, we are not going to go down without a fight," Jenna roared just as the Bofors cannon began to rattle off rounds. The machine fired into the water, not accurate enough or useful enough at such close quarters to take down individual arms. The CIWS also pushed rounds into the water, as the *Stratton* made it rain lead.

The boat came alive with every crew member that was in a non-essential position charging out onto the decks to engage their attacker. The sound of M16's, M870P's, and the two .50 calibre guns began to bark their tune of war.

The smaller limbs danced in the air, weaving around most of the heavy fire that came their way, but unable to dodge everything. Jenna watched as one of the smaller tentacles got torn in half by a spray of .50 fire. The limb severed with a sickeningly wet rip. Black blood spurted high into the air from the severed limb, spraying like a fire hose over the *Stratton*'s deck.

The severed section fell into the water with a crash, but the remaining stump continued to fight. It swept down onto the boat, slamming into the rear, making the craft lurch in the water. Several crew members were sent off balance, and that was when the other arms stuck. Two stabbed across the deck, piercing as many as five men each before they rose into the air and shook them loose. The bodies tore apart at the joints from the frantic waving. The rich red blood of human life fell like rain, spattering into the puddles of black sea monster blood.

"Push us to maximum speed," Jenna called as something crunched beneath the boat. The craft gave another lurch, as two more arms came sweeping in from either side to crush the sides of the craft.

Sirens began to wail, and people cried out as they were sent flying. Men fell overboard, their weapons still firing as they fell into the now rabid-looking ocean.

"We've lost power in one engine," someone spoke up, as they worked frantically to keep the craft alive.

"We have a hull breach. We are taking on water," another equally shaky voice came through the speakers.

Another slimy arm crashed against the front of the bridge. Jenna just had time to throw herself to the floor as it crashed through, shearing away the roof and upper walls. The cry of snapping metal and shattering glass was deafening. Jenna felt hot shards of both slice through her neck and hands as she lay there. Jumping to her feet, pulling her M16 into action, she unloaded on the sweeping tentacle, tearing a deep, long gash along its rear.

"Bulldog," she called out when she saw the man lying on the floor, his face a red mess of blood.

"I'm alive," he growled, hauling himself to his feet, crimson fluid leaking from the multiple lacerations that covered his face.

"We need to radio for support. The ship is lost. Get us out of here," Jenna ordered as she turned to survey the scene. Only her and Bulldog had survived the attack on the bridge. Around her, the bodies of her crew lay scattered over the floor. Not one body remained in one piece. Two heads and one arm lay at her feet, having rolled towards her as the boat once again lurched under the power of an underwater impact.

She saw Richard Green's body lying on the floor, his broken legs pointing towards the sky while his torso lay face down on the other side of the bridge. Intestines and all manner of organs snaked their way between the two halves, as if they were a spring and the young man could simply be pushed back together again.

"Choppers are being scrambled, but they're ten minutes out," Bulldog said as he white-knuckle gripped his weapon.

"Let's do this, Bulldog. We go down swinging," Jenna said as she strode to the edge of the bridge and began to fire at anything that moved.

She emptied her magazine into the belly of one of the larger tentacles, splitting it through the middle to such a degree she could see the horizon through the gash. Black blood rained down on the deck in a deluge, covering the remaining men with even more gore.

Their numbers had been severely depleted with bodies being plucked into the air and tossed around like dolls, thrown from one tentacle to the other.

"This fucking thing is playing with us," Bulldog roared above the growl of his M16.

He pulled out the empty magazine and slammed a fresh one home, his trigger finger letting up for just long enough to let the change happen.

The deck was wiped clean by the time the aerial assault from the approaching HH-65 Dolphins struck. The two choppers came in hot, with their M240 guns blazing. They tore through the tentacles that whipped wildly back and forth, trying to swat their new prey from the skies. The Dolphins were quite the match for the flailing appendages, and soon managed to drive them back below the surface for the first time since the skirmish began.

Quickly lowering towards the boat, the remaining survivors scurried up into the choppers as quick as they could. Bulldog and Jenna were the last two to be plucked from the deck of the rapidly sinking ship.

"Pull us up, now!" Jenna screamed at the pilot as she saw the water around the boat begin to darken and bubble.

The pilot did not hesitate. He too saw the signs, and hauled his bird into a steep climb, and moments later, the second chopper did the same.

The water erupted around the boat, as the creature's massive jaws powered from the water, its bird-like beak swallowing the craft whole before closing with a snap that created a rush of wind that had both Dolphin pilots fighting to keep control.

Bulldog grabbed the M240 and began to rattle off the rounds, but they simply bounced off the creature's iron-like outer beak with the only result being a small spark where the bullet ricocheted off its target.

"What the hell was that?" the pilot called as their choppers turned and moved back to the coast.

"A sea monster," Jenna panted as she sat back in the seat and said a silent prayer that she was still alive.

She looked over at Bulldog. He lay back in his seat while the co-pilot addressed the worst of his wounds. Blood covered his face, pumping from a nasty head wound that stretched over the top of his skull. The skin pulled back in a flap, like a poorly fitted toupee in the wind.

Jenna smiled, she couldn't help herself. They had survived. Barely. The fight cost her ninety percent of her crew. This fact pissed her off more than anything, and she made a promise to the dead that she would see to it that she got to take part in whatever operation got put together to hunt the beast.

CHAPTER 8

Pete, Randolph and Forrest set out early, making the drive up to the Mayport Naval Installation. They were greeted at the gate and escorted through to the office of Captain Ross McCall. He was a friendly man with a thick moustache and short, neatly trimmed hair. Flecks of great peppered both, and the creases that ran around the corners of his eyes and mouth when he smiled made him look more like a grandfather than a senior officer on a naval base.

"Captain, thank you for seeing us," Randolph began.

"My pleasure, please coming and take a seat. That will be all, thank you," Captain McCall spoke to the two young NCOs that had escorted the three men across the base thus far.

Both men saluted, turned and left the room without saying a word.

"You must be Pete Colden. I read your file, you and Captain Wiseman here go back some way." Ross reached out and shook Pete's hand. His grip was as firm and his hands as large as a catcher's mitt.

"Yes, sir," Pete answered crisply. "The captain and I served together for many years. I retired a while back, but you never forget where you cover from."

"Agreed," Ross said then turned his attention to Forrest, who had tried hard to dress smart for the occasion, but his expensive suit did little to dampen the immediate impression made by the shock of white hair that consumed both the top and bottom of his head.

"Forrest Jones, pleasure to meet you, sir," Forrest offered his hand, which came close to matching the size of McCall's.

The two men held the grip a while, as they surveyed one another.

"Mr. Jones, it is a pleasure to have you on this base. I will admit, that when the call first came through, I waved it off as being nonsense. Then I read the jackets of these two men, and my interest was piqued. I had no intentions of allowing a civilian onto my base, and certainly not in my own quarters to be party to such discussions, but in light of recent events, I realize that I was wrong in my initial assumption. As long as you are involved in this project, you will be treated as an officer of the Navy. This order has been given, and if anybody gives you any problems, report to me and I will ensure it is rectified," Captain McCall said as he rose from his chair and walked to the liquor cabinet. He came back with four glasses of scotch.

A small measure of amber liquid over two ice cubes. Each man took a glass and sat nursing it.

"I will admit, it is a little early, but as I said, recent events have been disturbing, to say the least," the captain said as he sipped his drink.

"Recent events?" Randolph asked.

He was not the only one to have heard the repeated phrase.

"Yes, you see we just got word that the *USCGC Stratton* has just been lost off the coast," Captain McCall began.

"Lost as in …" Pete asked, knowing that a single word can be interpreted in many ways.

"I think the most accurate word I could think of would be, eaten. Something ate a four-hundred foot long US Coastguard Clipper." Captain McCall let that hang in the air for a while.

He took another sip of his drink and watched as the other three men did the same.

"How many did we lose?" Randolph asked, his voice as heavy as his heart.

"There were fifty-seven people on board, we pulled seven off the boat before it sank. Three of those are in critical condition, and between you and me, I don't think they are going to make it," McCall said, the emotion thick in his voice.

"Shit," Randolph exhaled as he sank back into the sofa.

"It was the Kraken, wasn't it?" Forrest spoke. He held his empty glass up to his face and continued to swirl the ice cubes around, watching them dance inside the fat receptacle.

"I don't know, but if that is what you want to call this monster, then that works for me. All I know is that there is something out in the water that is a danger to all of us." Captain McCall sat back on the chair, not relaxing into it, but simply pushing himself further onto the seat.

"We need to stop it," Pete began.

"If you know how, then I am all ears, because this one is close to home and anything we do, especially in this day and age, is going to be all over the news before we even make the announcement." The strain was already beginning to show on McCall.

"We came close once before, back in eighty-three," Pete said.

"We hit it with everything at our disposal. Didn't kill it, we did enough damage to force the beast into hiding," Randolph spoke up to give some substance to Pete's claims.

"You put it to sleep, or rather, it put itself to sleep. It matured," Forrest spoke up. "An oil company woke it up, and now that it's fully grown, it is going to take something large to stop it."

"What do you have in mind?" Captain McCall asked, looking at the old man with interest.

"I'm not a military man. I'm not a gun lobbyist. I hate the damned things. The how I will gladly leave up to you. I've spent my whole life reading about this creature. I still know diddly-squat, but I bet it's more than you," Forrest answered, placing the glass onto the table.

"We will need to launch a strike against it," Pete said. "The only way to get rid of it, is to find it and blow it out of the water."

"I agree with you, but the public perception is something that must always be considered," Captain McCall answered.

"The public perception won't matter much at all if we don't take this thing out." Pete stood his ground. "Who even knows how big this thing is, or what it is really capable of? I mean, it has taken down an oil rig, a cutter-class ship, and I saw it take down multiple fishing vessels at the same time."

"I understand, nobody wants to get rid of this threat more than I do. However, we need to do it in the right way. This remains my station, and

I remain the man who calls the shots." McCall began to growl, his voice telling them that he was not going to be pushed around. "I have extended a courtesy to the three of you, you are here under my approval, and you would be well served to remember that, especially as a civilian."

Pete said nothing and sat back down on the sofa. For a while, nobody spoke.

"We need to find out where it is. We need to understand how it acts and try to gauge just how big it is," Forrest said, bored by the silence. The entertainment offered by the three old servicemen comparing the size of their dicks only lasted so long.

"I thought you were the expert," Pete shot viciously.

"I know what I know through research. I last saw this creature in the seventies, and only got close to it once and that was over sixty years ago. I think we need a more relevant source. Somebody who knows this creature better than any of us," Forrest answered them, his green eyes moving from man to man, watching their responses.

"What are you suggesting?" Captain McCall asked.

"We need to speak with the people rescued off that Coast Guard ship." Forrest sat back and clasped his hands over one another. While he held no hidden inclination to be some brave bold leader, but he would not sit about idly while others argued about nothing.

CHAPTER 9

Lieutenant Jenna Harrington passed out on the flight back to the short. She woke in Saint Jude's Hospital. Her injuries were not as severe as those of some of her colleagues. However, the medical staff decided to hold her for forty-eight hours, just for observation. Jenna didn't mind, especially when they wheeled her into a private room. She only had one neighbour, a heavily sedated and stitched up Bulldog Brown. The doctors agreed to give her regular updates on his condition, and Jenna made sure they had the contact details for Bulldog's wife and kids.

She tried to visit him twice, but each time, the doctors and nurses shooed her away, their updates being the only courtesy extended to her. For the rest, they seemed intent on keeping them separated. No doubt the injured men babbling about sea monsters put the staff on high alert.

Jenna was smart; she refused to give any details as to what transpired on the boat, saving her testimony for the panel that she felt certain would be waiting for her upon her release. The doctors saved the lives of her crew, but at the end of the day, still lacked the clearance level to be given all of the unfiltered details.

Life in the military was difficult, and Jenna made the decision early in her career that a family, a husband and kids, would have to wait until after she finished active duty. She dated but did not allow herself the change to form a relationship that could be considered even vaguely serious, or even serious adjacent. Her family lived in the north-west, and given her career choice and shore time, she did not get the chance to visit them very often. She came from a close family, and while they spoke regularly, life's habit of ruining the best-laid plans meant it had been several years since Jenna last visited them for any lengthy period of time. She was surprised, therefore, when the nurse arrived to announce that she had three visitors waiting to see her.

"Only if you think you are up for it, otherwise I will send them away," the nurse said with a smile.

The Coast Guard representative had already been in and advised her to stay under observation and to report back to the division once she was released.

"Send them up," Jenna said, intrigued by who it could be.

"Sorry to disturb you," the first man said as he knocked on the door.

Jenna looked up from her chair and studied the men. There were three of them, one in military dress, a captain she saw, and immediately went to stand at attention.

"At ease, at ease, none of that nonsense right now," Randolph said as he walked into the room.

Behind him stood a shorter, tubbier man who looked as if he had spent far too long in the sun, his skin worn and leathered. Beside him stood an even short man, an older man, with the beginnings of a hunched back and a shock of white hair that threatened to consume his whole head, save for the eyes, piercing green eyes that she could feel studying her.

"Thank you," Jenna said. She would not admit it, but she was not feeling her best after the day she had had. "Who are you?"

"My name is Captain Randolph Wiseman, this here is an old buddy of mine Pete Colden, and that there is Forrest Jones, he is … I guess you could call him an expert." Randolph made no move to further enter the room. "We would like to talk to you about what happened today."

"I … I don't know what I can tell you," Jenna said, lowering her gaze.

"Just tell us everything you can. We know what you saw out there. Do not feel ashamed to speak of it." Forrest moved further into the room, and Jenna turned to look at him.

"What was that thing?" She felt close to tears.

"We don't know for sure. For the last sixty years, I called it the Kraken. Please, may I sit?" Forrest motioned to the unoccupied chair.

"Yes, please, I'm sorry, come in all of you." Jenna beckoned the others to join her and Forrest.

Jenna offered her chair to Randolph, but he refused, and so he and Pete sat on the edge of the hospital bed. Slowly, and gently, they walked through the events on the *Stratton*.

None of the men seemed keen to interrupt Jenna once she started talking, and so they let her tell her tale. They had questions, but they would come later.

By the time she finished talking, Jenna was worn out and sweating. Talking about the creature brought everything back to her. She closed her eyes, and when she opened them again, Randolph stood ready with a fresh tissue.

"Thank you. Would you look at me," Jenna said as she snorted a laugh.

"Don't feel bad. What you saw out there, what you survived, is something nobody can even contemplate," Forrest spoke, leaning forward to place a hand on her shoulder.

"Indeed, you faced this beast and survived. Not many can say that," Pete said from the bed. "If it is as large as you said, then it is an even greater feat."

"How are you going to stop it?" Jenna asked.

"That is something we have yet to figure out. You need to get some rest, we have taken up enough of your time already," Forrest said, rising to his feet as his back gave an audible pop.

"I'm coming with you," Jenna insisted.

"I'm afraid that will not be possible. You need your rest," Randolph began.

"Bullshit, sir," Jenna snapped and shot to her feet. "If anybody should be out there when that thing bites the big one, then it should be me." Her steel blue eyes were as cold as the metal they took their colouration from.

It was clear that Jenna had no intention to take no for an answer, especially when she pulled off her hospital gown and started dressing in front of the men.

"Hold on, I really don't advise you getting out of bed. That is an order, Lieutenant," Randolph bellowed, his voice rising in a way that seemed to boom through the entire room. "Now we were here for a friendly chat, but if you want to make this something else, then I will pull rank on you. You are going to get back into bed, and finish your observation period."

"But—" Jenna began and Randolph silenced her with a raised hand.

"But, once you have been discharged, report to Mayport Base. I give you my word that you will be allowed to join us when we hunt this beast. If you still feel the same way that is." Randolph's voice returned to normal and he finished his speech with a friendly smile.

Jenna said nothing for a moment. She held her ground, with her shirt pulled over her head but only one arm positioned correctly.

"You should listen to him," Pete offered. "There is no arguing with him once his mind is made up."

"Fine, but I want to be involved in this. That thing killed my team, and I want its blood."

"You shall have it, Lieutenant," Randolph spoke and guided her back to bed.

As they left the room, a nurse near ran up to them. They saw the pensive look on her face and immediately feared the worst for the Chief Petty Officer Brown.

"I'm glad I caught you before you left," the nurse spoke. She was a large, Hispanic woman with dark-tanned skin and a pretty face.

"What's wrong?" Forrest asked, studying the woman.

"Somebody tipped off the media and now there is a real storm brewing out there." She looked around as she spoke, as if she expected some nosey reporter to be found snooping around the corner.

"Thank you," Randolph said.

"You can leave through the back, the ambulance bay," she added with a smile.

Pete turned and started walking, and Randolph extended his hand to the nurse, who took it and smiled once more.

The two old Navy friends turned and started to walk down the corridor, as from the other direction, the clamour of reporters echoed their way.

"Wait, what about the lieutenant?" Forrest asked.

The two men stopped, but only Randolph turned around, he looked at Forrest and understood what he meant.

"Nurse?" he asked.

The nurse was also no dummy and was already nodding her head. "She should stay for observation, but I saw her charts, she has no serious injuries."

"Perfect, Forrest, will you go and tell the lieutenant that she can—"

"No need, I'm already ready," Jenna spoke, appearing in the doorway fully dressed and moving.

CHAPTER 10

The guard that stopped the car looked sceptical when he saw the fourth member of their group. She had not been with them when they left the base, and it didn't sit well with him. However, one of the men inside the car was a captain, and it was far beyond his pay grade to question the moves and motives of an officer of such rank.

Seaman Richards opened the gates and let the car pass, watching them as they drove away.

Something was happening, and the silence that surrounded it did not sit well with Richards. There had been a flurry of activity already that morning. More unexpected arrivals than he could remember in the last several months combined. Not to mention the fact that there were whisperings among those in the barracks that something big was going down.

Randolph drove the men straight to the captain's room on the base and handed the keys of the military vehicle back to the same warrant officer they had taken them from. The young man, whose uniform identified him as Mutch, saluted the group as they approached.

"Sir, will you be needing the vehicle again, sir?" The man was crisp and well starched in his pose.

"No, thank you, I believe we are done with that for today," Randolph answered.

Captain McCall was waiting for them, and he was not alone in his room. Two other men both dressed in the uniform of the Coast Guard turned and addressed the group that entered.

"I did not realize I had sent you on a rescue mission, Captain Wiseman," Captain McCall spoke, his tone one that made it hard to gauge if he was being serious or sarcastic.

"Yes, things did not really go according to plan," Randolph answered.

"Do enlighten us."

"Somebody tipped off the media, and we thought, given how you were concerned about public image and social media, getting the lieutenant here out of their path was in the best interest of all," Pete answered, his retired status giving him a little leverage when it came to the level of snark allowed in his responses.

"Very well, I appreciate the thought." This time, McCall did smile, and the atmosphere in the room changed.

Between the men, Jenna stood silent. She knew better than to speak out of turn, especially when she was not on her own base.

"Good to see you up and about, Lieutenant. I understand that it was your quick thinking that saved the lives of your crew this morning," Captain McCall spoke.

"Thank you, sir, but—"

"I understand what you are going through. You did not save them all, and that weighs heavy on you. It is the problem of the battlefield. Every loss is felt by the people in charge, but we are not often afforded the time, in the moment, to let it show," McCall interrupted, his words reassuring and soft.

"Your actions did not go unnoticed today, Lieutenant," one of the two other men spoke.

"Thank you, sir," Jenna said, raising her gaze to meet that of the man who had addressed her.

"Gentlemen," Captain McCall resumed talking. "Allow me to introduce Captain Dwight Henderson and Master Chief Alistair Elmers."

Captain Henderson was a man who immediately fitted in with the other men of his age and rank. His jet black hair had the same intense shade as in high school, and his jaw was sharp and strong. When he shook hands, the muscles in his forearms popped.

The master chief was different. He was young, and had a youthfulness that reduced his visual age somewhat dramatically. Tall with broad shoulders and bright blue eyes, he looked the poster child for the US forces.

Elmers' eyes locked on Jenna, and he smiled. His teeth were a brilliant white and movie star straight. Jenna returned the smile and felt herself flush just a little. "Nice to meet you, Lieutenant," He spoke with a soft, deep voice.

"I wish our meeting here could have been under better circumstances, but I fear there is no time to be lost in inter-force congenialities," McCall began.

"What happened?" Pete asked.

"Our monster is back," Forrest spoke. He had not said much since they left the hospital, but over the years, he taught himself a great measure of restraint. Listening proved to be a much greater weapon than talking, and ensured that when he did speak, every word counted.

"Indeed, Mr. Jones," Captain McCall said with a smirk. "We have intercepted multiple reports coming in of strange occurrences up and down the coast. Boats are being thrown through the water, fishermen are having their nets and rods destroyed ..." McCall explained before a knock at the door cut him off.

"Sir, the meeting room is all set up and ready for you," a young seaman spoke confidently.

"Thank you," the captain answered. "Shall we?"

They moved through the connecting door from the captain's office and into a large meeting room. An oval-shaped table occupied the central space. Its dark wood was polished to a high-definition shine. Places had been set to account for each of them, including Jenna. That fact was not lost on either Forrest or Randolph, but both knew enough than to pass comment on it.

"Gentlemen," McCall began. "We are up against a threat that we do not understand. Something that cannot easily be labelled as an enemy, but very simple as a monster. We have several people in this room who had seen the beast, and that fact alone is enough for me to conquer my own scepticism. Recent events have confirmed this in my mind, and now the time has come for us to make a move against this beast before even more people have to die." There was silence around the table as McCall spoke.

He pressed a button, and a projector descended from the ceiling, taking its merry time doing so. In the intervening silence, each of them took the chance to fill their water glasses, with the master chief offering to fill Jenna's for her, and she blushed as she accepted the offer.

"As I mention, we have had multiple reports coming in of strange events and even one of two sightings that are causing us quite some concern." A map of the Florida coast appeared, and as the captain spoke, red crosses appeared, indicating the various locations of the events.

They started down beyond the keys, moved out to sea before sweeping back inland towards the coast.

"As you can see, the creature is moving towards the more heavily populated areas. We assume this to be because of the food source, but at this point in time, everything we have to go on is pure speculation."

"If that thing wanted to eat, it would. It does. I think it is playing with us. Right now, it is toying with what it finds." Forrest did not wait for his turn to speak, he simply interrupted the flow and brought all eyes around to him.

"Upon what grounds do you make that statement?" Captain Henderson snapped. "I think you will find it certainly ate my men."

Forrest said nothing for a few moments. He did not like Henderson. The man's tones and approach to things did not match his own viewpoint. Around the room, the wood panelling shone, its finish as equally highly polished as the table. Various portraits of previous admirals and members of the military hierarchy stared down on them. The carpet beneath the feet was a deep blue, and the finish of the wall above the wood was white. Everything was neat, crisp and clean.

"That is exactly my point, Captain." Forrest paused, thinking before he spoke. "That creature took out several boats, an oil rig and your vessel while it was enraged. It was woken, disturbed and threatened."

Captain Henderson opened his mouth to interrupt, but Forrest continued talking, raising his tone just enough to let them know he had seen the attempt, and did not appreciate it, or plan on acknowledging it.

"I was out on the water the other night, and I witnessed it feeding. It drove the fish to the surface and just scooped them inside. What is happening now, that is not hunger, nor rage, this monster is playing with us, plain and simple."

"You make it sound like we are dealing with a child," the master chief spoke up.

"I have no idea, we could be, or maybe an adolescent. It is all just guesswork, all I am trying to say is that we are not just hunting some hungry monster," Forrest corrected. "Don't get me wrong, I think we can all agree that this thing needs to be stopped, and we will not do that sitting around a table. So I suggest we cut through this nonsense and get to the important part of the conversation. How do you plan on killing this monster?"

CHAPTER 11

Nate Stanley sat in the helicopter as below him the coast gave way to the ocean, the white sand replaced by the azure of the Atlantic Ocean. Up there with him was his cameraman, Harry Holmes. The Enstrom F-28 helicopter shook and rattled as they began their wild goose chase. Nate had initially refused to take the assignment. He had yelled at his producer, wasting no effort in telling her that just because he had refused her most recent drunken booty call, he had no intention of suffering the indignity of a monster hunt.

Nate and his producer, Susan, had been involved in a rather nasty love affair for the past several years. Both had minor drinking problems, and had woken up after many a late-night session with their naked, sweat-covered bodies entwined, stuck together with the fluids of their passion.

Susan was married, with her poor, clueless husband too busy working and raising their family to have even the most remote idea of his wife's wild slutty side.

The affair was abusive, with both having often taken blows from the other during their rampant and destructive fuck sessions. Neither proclaimed to have any true feelings for the other. Everything they did either driven by drink, drugs, or an erotic combination of the way, and fuelled by a raw animalistic attraction.

Yet, as he gazed at the ocean, mesmerized by the smooth changing shade the further they moved from the coast, Nate realized two things. Susan had played him, flirting with him, ignoring his rage and seducing him into agreeing to take the report. The second was that his hatred for her had risen to a new height, one that could only be attained based on a more substantial emotion that ran even deeper.

"This is the spot," Harry said as he pulled the chopper around in a wide arc. Beneath them, the water was flat and empty, about as boring as one could possibly imagine for a news report.

"Are you sure? There's nothing down there, man," Nate snorted.

"Sorry, dude, this is the spot. I don't like it any more than you do. So let's get this record, move on to the next place and get back down in time to grab a breakfast burger before they stop serving them." Harry grabbed his camera and began to work on both getting the camera rolling and holding the chopper steady.

"Alright, but you're buying."

"Deal, and we are live in three … two …" Before Harry had the chance to finish his count, the chopper spun out of control.

The feed went live regardless, and the audience was greeted to the sight of a lead reporter screaming, as the chopper spun around and around. Alarms bells sounded, but the shouts and screams of the two man crew drowned them out.

"What the hell is that?"

"Sweet Jesus, help us."

Both men called and cried out as something thick and brown slid into view. The tentacle whipped back and forth in a shower of blood. There was a wet, gargling cry and a headless Nate sat before the camera, his headset resting on the bloody stump of his neck.

A few moments later, the feed cut out, preceded by a loud crunch, and a few seconds later, an explosion.

Harry was frozen, not only through fear, but from the tentacle that had wrapped around his body. It pulled him into the seat, crushing him. Pain consumed him as he felt multiple sets of jaws chew through his flesh and into his body. Blood flowed from the wounds coating the slimy, foul smelling limb with gore. Harry was still alive when the feed finally broke. He was still alive when an inquisitive tentacle extended up to the Enstrom F-28 rotor blades. The limb exploded in a shower of black gelatinous blood, which coated Harry like goo.

The rotors flew in different directions, and the main fuselage dropped as the limbs withdrew, following their mangled counterpart, sinking back into the ocean.

Harry was alive as the craft plummeted, and hit the water. He was dead by the time the breast tore him and the craft apart in its rage.

FLTV did not have the high viewer ratings or a national channel, but its audience was more than enough viewers to have witnessed the live attack to send fear reverberating through the public. Word of mouth began and soon the internet came alive with the report, and with that came the problems people like Captain McCall and those above his head had been trying to avoid.

CHAPTER 12

"We need to do something," Randolph spoke up.

The group was still sitting in the meeting room, having just sat through the fifth replay of the news report. The reports coming in were of sightings up and down the coast. Everything from dolphins and manatees to a school of tuna and mahi-mahi were being reported as sea monsters. Descriptions also ranged from the more accurate octopus and squid variants, to the utterly insane, merpeople and Hydras, not to mention the reported confirmations from a beach-fronted religious community that the creature was a leviathan coming to punish us for our sins and usher in a new age of religious consciousness.

"We have helicopters en-route, if they see anything, they will engage. The number one priority right now is to move this creature away from the populated areas," Captain Henderson spoke.

While the others had been studying the video, he had taken decisive action.

"We have two MH-60's in the air. Their ETA to the spot where that chopper went down is six minutes." He read from his tablet, which relayed all of the real-time information he needed.

"We need more than just a few helicopters," Forrest addressed the group, but his eyes were settled on Captain McCall. "We need to get some subs and cruisers, and shit out there. We need to fight, not dance around."

"If things were that simple, Mr. Jones, then do you not think we would have done that already?" the captain snapped, clearly not in the mood to be second guessed.

"I understand, but looking at how this thing has behaved, the research I have done over the years, I just don't think you want to piss this thing off," Forrest continued, determined to hold his ground.

"You might want to listen to the man," Randolph began.

Captain McCall's face darkened like the sky before a storm. His eyes seemed to bulge as he tried hard to contain himself.

"What gives you the right to tell me how to run my operations?" He glared at Forrest. "You are a civilian to whom I have extended a very generous courtesy. I would expect a little bit of professionalism from a man who—"

"A man who what, chases monsters for a living? A man who become an orphan after this beast ripped his family apart? I know more about that beast than you do, and considering how vague most information is out there, you ought to be listening to me." Forrest raised his voice, and in a rare moment of rage indulgence, he allowed his words to flow without a filter.

"I think we are all aware of the situation." Randolph stood up.

"I would agree. With all due respect, Mr. Jones, the decisions here are to be made by those in charge. We understand your dedication, and appreciate your input. I'm sure you understand that sending out so many vessels would be viewed as a very aggressive act, and with Cuba so close to all of this, there are some very tricky questions that we will need to prepare answers for. Allow us the chance to operate surveillance on this creature, and then, when the time is right, our further action will be thought out and justified," the master chief spoke.

His words came straight from the textbook. Well delivered and heartfelt. They did not work on Forrest the way they were supposed to, but he did back down, because he understood the potential issues. Yet, he was determined not to let the matter drop.

CHAPTER 13

Ben Saunders had seen the news broadcast. He had actually been watching live. He had also been fully briefed on the matter at hand. He was under strict orders to engage the beast should the creature be seen.

He, along with another pilot, and his long-term friend, Matthew Grey, had been tasked with driving the creature away from the coast into deeper water.

Ben, a fourteen-year veteran, had seen and done a great many things, but chasing a sea monster was by far and above the most unusual. He was excited to take to the skies and chase the son of a bitch down, as wrong as it sounded to be excited about taking a life. Who doesn't want to go out and catch a genuine monster? Calling the creature the Kraken had been an instantaneous decision. Pure coincidence that the three men sitting with Captain McCall used the same name for the beast. After all, what else could you call a large-tentacled sea beast? Matthew had argued a good case for Cthulhu, but both agreed that seemed a little too far-fetched, not to mention, harder to pronounce.

Each helicopter had a gunman on-board. The two men, young fresh faces not long out of academy, sat in identical positions, rigid and ready for action from the moment the birds left the ground. Their seriousness stark against the contrast of the older pilots.

Boats crowded the otherwise calm sea. The on-air death of a news reporter was widely regarded as one of the largest tragedies, and certainly ranking up in the level of the Christine Chubbuck incident. However, the fact that a sea monster was responsible had been enough to bring people flocking to the water.

The crowded beaches were even more densely populated than normal, everybody standing along the water's edge, hoping to get a glimpse of the beast. The water, too, was likewise densely overpopulated. Boats of all shapes and sizes moved through the water.

They lacked any real direction, but all seemed intent on keeping their position. Everybody from hunters keen to claim the scalp of the murdering beast through to photographers and nature-loving hippies had decided to throw caution to the wind.

"Clearly none of these fools has ever seen Jaws," Matthew spoke from one bird to another.

"I know, we need to keep them in mind. If we have to engage too close to the coast, then these guys could be a real problem," Ben answered. "You hold on tight back there, don't fire until I give the word. The last thing we need is friendly fire taking out a few nut jobs."

"Yes, sir," the young seaman answered.

"I'm no sir, kid. Save that kind of talk for those that deserve it," Ben said with a smile. Even after fourteen years, he could still remember the stale rigidity of being a fresh recruit.

The choppers moved in the same direction, but at a distance that gave them both expanded visibility up and down the coast, as well as enough room to manoeuvre should the unthinkable happen.

"I've got something, twelve o'clock," Matthew spoke up, his voice all business.

"Confirmed, I have visual," Ben said, hearing his gunner take a sharp breath.

"You go take a look. We will circle back and cover you if needed." Ben gave the order and Matthew listened. While the two men were both of identical rank, their natural personalities and close bond had them both understanding who was best to take charge in any given situation.

Beside them, the other chopper adjusted its course and headed out to sea, coming up on the object from an angle. He waited and then pulled his bird around to follow. He smiled as he moved in, closing the distance. His heart was racing, but he felt calm and ready as he moved his bird around.

"The sensors are not picking up a thing," Matthew reported as he reached the mass.

"Just keep your wits about you," Ben answered as he closed the distance between him and the lead chopper.

The mass in the sea was a large black cloud floating on the surface, or just beneath, it was difficult to tell. The wind from the sixteen meter long rotors kicked up a multitude of small white-capped waves.

"I don't know what I'm looking at, but it ain't no sea monster," the young gunner behind Ben spoke as they turned a circle over the substance.

"Looks like oil," Ben agreed.

"Or ink," Matthew said, just as a long tentacle shot from the water and licked at his bird.

"Matt, behind you," Ben called, and his friend reacted without thought, pulling up hard on the stick, hauling the chopper into a steep climb. The gunner lost his footing and slid out of the open side door. He caught hold of himself at the last minute, his legs dangling out of the helicopter like a stuntman in an action movie.

"Sweet Christ," the seaman behind Ben cried out.

"What are you fucking waiting for? Shoot!" Ben roared as he swung his helicopter around to bring the gun in line with the water.

"I don't see—"

"Just shoot!" Ben yelled without letting the young man finish.

The roll of the M240 rang out like a war cry spitting out close to a thousand rounds a minute, turning the sea into a bubbling turmoil. The tentacles disappeared back beneath waves.

"Sensors are still giving me nothing," Matthew's voice came from the descending helicopter.

"I don't know, but we need to drive that fucker away from those boats," Ben spoke.

Behind them, an armada of sparkling white boats charged towards the action. Eager fools desperate to get up close to the monster, to witness man overcoming the beast.

"What the living fuck are they doing?" Matthew growled.

"Getting themselves killed." Ben turned his chopper around and headed towards the boats, flying down low over the water, buzzing the front line.

"Let loose, kid, just don't hit them," he instructed his young and nervous gunman.

"But …"

"Just trust me," Ben insisted.

The kid pulled the trigger, and a fresh chain of ammo fired into the water. The speed of the rounds pummelling the surface from such close distance created a wall of water and shot up from the surface. Ben flew along the line of boats, who heeded his warning and had stopped their advance.

"It's working. They are backing down," the gunman reported.

Ben gave him no answer. Their warning had not been the reason the boats had stopped. The long, spreading shadow appeared beneath the water, snaking limbs that moved under the surface like lightning.

The tentacles shot into the air and grabbed at the chopper. They wrapped around the struts and pulled them free with the grating crunch of shearing metal.

"I can't get a shot," the young man screamed.

"I'm trying, kid," Ben grunted as he wrestled for control of the rotorcraft.

Bullets tore through the grappling tentacle, slicing through flesh, sending the injured limb retreating into the water, while the severed end continued to crawl and grab at the underside of the helicopter.

Ben swung the helicopter around in a tight circle, throwing the limb free. It flew through the air, landing in the midst of the gathered boats, which had now decided the panic and cause even more congestion on the water.

The limb landed in one boat and immediately wrapped itself around the leg of the occupant. Within seconds, the craft was slick with blood and ink. The tentacle ate through the man's leg and sent him sprawling.

The unmanned boat careered on a rough and unsteady course crashing into a larger vessel which tipped and spilled into the water.

"Fire," Ben roared, and both aircraft unloaded with their mounted machineguns. One thousand, two, three, four then five thousand rounds pummelled the water, the choppers holding steady over the water, pummelling the same spot over and over. The water bubbled like a hot tub on full power from the non-stop barrage, the water bubbling first white and then black, as they tore into the body of the beast.

"That's right, you son of a bitch," the young gunner behind Ben roared as his belt emptied and the weapon began to click.

The water below them became a spreading pool of black. The water surface was calming after the onslaught.

"Damn good shooting. What's you name again, seaman?" Ben asked his young partner

"Terrence, Terrence Yorke."

"Good work. I'll make sure they all know how you did," Ben said. He was watching the sea, waiting, expecting some form of attack, but no retaliating strike came. "Hey, you OK back there?"

Terrence gave no answer. Ben positioned himself to turn around when his gunner appeared beside him. The only problem being he was on the outside of the chopper. Something thrust the young man's face against the side of the craft with enough force to split his skull down the middle like a coconut. The crack ran through his forehead and down to the bridge of his nose. Blood and brain matter leaked from the young man's shattered skull as the tentacle wrapped further and further around the body, squeezing until the head burst from the shoulders with such a force the pilot's window shattered. The severed head landed in Ben's lap, the eyes staring up at him.

Ben pulled on the stick, ignoring the severed head in his crotch, but it was too late. The tentacles surged into the cockpit and wrapped through and around the chopper, moving underneath, staying away from the rotor blades.

A heavy pressure crushed against Ben's chest with enough force to make his vision starry. Great blotches of black appeared like the negatives of a camera flash. Pain consumed him and his hands fell from the controls. He could feel the life being sucked out of him by the hungry mouths that were the suction cups on the tentacles underside.

Guns fired as Ben realized Matthew was coming his way. The helicopter headed straight for them, the M240 unloading on the target.

Then everything began to spin. The world turned and tumbled, as the creature launched the chopper through the air. With his body all but exhausted, Ben was helpless to resist as he rapidly closed ground on the approaching helo.

There was no time to react. Everything happened in an instant. The two helicopters collided mid-air. Ben snapped forward in his seat as the front of his craft sheared into the front of Matthew's. Metal impacted metal with a screech that made the surviving men's eardrums burst. The whirring rotors collided and spinning shards flew in all directions, peppering the scrambling fleet of retreating boats. Bodies fell as they were cut in half by the twirling shrapnel.

The helicopter bodies meshed together upon impact, caught up in a lovers embrace as they spun down and into the ocean. Black, inky water rushed into the roughly fused fuselages. Matthew's gunner, Scott Carlson, was long dead, his upper body washed out to sea while his legs lay on opposite ends of the cabins base. Matthew was alive when they hit the water. He tried to move, but his belt and everything were jammed. Metal had pierced his legs, pinning him to the seat. He could do nothing but thrash around in terror as the cabin filled with water. Matthew coughed and gagged as water filled his lungs, and with a final choke, he was gone.

CHAPTER 14

The men were still locked in the same meeting room when the news came that both choppers had been lost, destroyed by the beast.

Captain McCall was angry. His face darkening, moving through different shades of red until it reached the deep colour of beetroot. The first person to get in his way stood in line for an ass chewing unlike anything seen before.

Forrest sat in silence, his head bowed. He thought about the lives that had been lost and his anger grew. He had told them that nothing short of an all-out offensive would have been any good. Nobody listened to him. They never did.

Pete and Randolph sat in silence. They stared at the large projector screen and studied the map of the eastern seaboard.

Jenna had her head bowed, doing her best to hide her tears as she wept for another round of lost colleagues.

Beside her, the master chief sat with a look of stony concentration etched into his remarkably handsome features. He held a tablet in his hands, and every now and then, his fingers pecked at the touchscreen. Captain Henderson was pacing the room, his hand was scratching at his chin. He would stop from time to time behind the master chief, as if checking on his work.

A long time passed before anybody spoke. Too long.

"We need to do something, Captain," Randolph spoke up. Being of equal rank to the other men in the room, he was best placed to give comment.

"I tried to warn you," Forrest spoke, spitting the words under his breath but loud enough for everybody to hear.

"What did you say, civilian?" Captain McCall froze on the spot, his eyes burning holes into the old man.

"I warned you. I told you that sending two helicopters would only piss her off. Well congratulations, mission accomplished. She's mad now. This is not some problem we can just ignore. This creature is old, strong, and from what we have seen so far, still growing."

Captain McCall looked at him, a vein bulged on the side of his neck. "What would you propose, civilian? This is the US Navy, not some group of misbegotten ghost chasers. We cannot invest millions of dollars chasing after the loch ness fucking monster. We would be the laughing stock of the world." His voice boomed and resonated through the room. Yet nobody flinched.

"Excuse me, Captain McCall, but this creature is not Nessie. This thing is a killing machine. How many more of your men need to die before you realize that we need to play the role of the aggressor?" Forrest turned his eyes from Captain McCall to Captain Henderson and then back again. "That in itself is grounds for war, surely to God. This creature will not stop. I have tracked this beast over the globe in the past half century, longer than that. She will not stop of her own accord. The Navy sanctioned an attack last time, and they were close. This time, with today's machines, we could kill that thing outright. Let the world know. This changes the game as far as I am concerned." Forrest sat back and felt all eyes move from him to Captain McCall, as if they were watching a game of tennis, following the conversational ball back and forth.

Captain McCall stared at Forrest, but ultimately he sat back down in his chair at the head of the oval table, placed his elbows before him interlocked his fingers and rested his chin on top. He let out a long sigh.

"I want boats in the water. I want to know where this thing is, and I want it dead."

The base turned into a frantic hive of activity as everybody scurried about, listening to the various orders that were coming in from here, there and everywhere. To Forrest, a bystander and foreign to the workings of the military, the scene looked chaotic, but he told himself the reality had to be much different. He glanced over at the faces of Randolph and even Pete, who even after all this time, was still more military at the core. They gave nothing away, their eyes studying the movement of the troops with as much fascination as Forrest.

Captain McCall disappeared, leaving his guests to their own devices, while the three officers from the Coast Guard had been whisked away, no doubt onto a ship ready to head out into battle.

"I hope they are right about this," Pete said as they stood staring at the small strike group as they left the base.

Two submarines, the *Wyoming* and the *Alaska*, led the charge. Neither sub was part of the permanent force at Mayport, but happened to be docked temporarily after the *Alaska* had required some repair work to various items of electrical equipment on the bridge.

Behind them came the cruisers, *Gettysburg* and *Vicksburg,* and the destroyer, *Lassen.* The five ships left the port, to no fanfare, no standing ovation and waving loved ones. They left quickly and quietly with only one objective, to kill the Kraken.

CHAPTER 15

Captain Clarence Merriweather stood on the bridge of the *Wyoming* and listened to the smooth running of this crew. An experienced captain at the twilight of his career, his crew considered him an easy-going man and a fair captain. His record was exemplary, having never received any form of discipline during his entire career, although he would be the first to admit that in his younger days, he had ridden lucks coattails on several occasions.

His XO, a young, up-and-coming lieutenant by the name of Ian Young, stood by his side. Their most recent deployment had been their first one together. After a few initial teething problems, they soon gelled, and for the latter half of the deployment, they functioned as a smooth-running team.

Ian had a tendency to be brash and over-zealous. He believed that the only secret to a good defence was an even more power offense. He had a lot to learn, but he was well respected throughout the Navy, and it was only a matter of time before he would receive his own command. Unlike many officers, he did not come from a military background. In fact, he came from a wealthy family. He was the very definition of a trust fund baby. He had walked away from the money to pursue the career he had dreamed about as far back as he could remember.

Ian's money ensured he endured several tough early years, but Ian had borne the suffering well, and became even more respected among his peers as a result.

The *Wyoming* took the lead as the group moved into a vague formation. Behind them, the *Alaska* followed close on their heel. Neither sub had felt the need to submerge.

***

"Hold her steady, we need to keep ahead of the ships, and I want an open comms channel through to the *Wyoming*." Captain Lance Douglas gave the orders.

"Yes, sir," his XO, Lieutenant Stuart Regal, barked his response.

Unlike their counterparts on the other submarine, the relationship between the captain and his XO was a much more old-school affair. The captain gave the orders and he expected everybody to listen to them and obey. Questions or alternatives that did not come from his own mouth were ignored and greeted with a stony silence and an angry glare that had been known to make many men shake in their shoes.

"I don't want that sub getting a trace more action than us. This is the *Alaska*, and we are the pride of our class." Captain Douglas addressed his crew with the same high and mighty way of thinking that they were used to.

While still a fair captain, Douglas ensured he ran a tight ship. Everybody knew not to act out of turn. A blind eye was never turned and there was not a man on his crew who had not been written up for something through the years.

The *Alaska* and *Wyoming* had both been briefed on what had happened and were aware of the destruction the creature had caused. They had also been told all about how the creature could essentially cloak itself.

"I want everybody at the ready. This creature could strike from anywhere, and I want its head on a plate before the end of the day," Douglas ordered, sitting in the captain's chair and smiling as his men busied themselves. He prided himself on the how smoothly his command functioned. His mind was already running a hundred miles an hour, filled with thoughts of the promotion he would get if he were to be the man that took down the beast. He was tired of being on a sub and had his eyes set on a nice position at a different base where just last week where a rear admiral had passed away somewhat unexpectedly.

***

"Sir, the subs are away," his XO, Amanda Jennings, announced. "Do we hold our current course or head out into deeper water, sir?"

"Hold our current course. I want to keep the subs close for a little while yet. This creature is out there, and we would be foolish to all rush in one after another," Captain Luke Stronghold answered.

The bridge of the *Gettysburg* was buzzing. They were the lead of the three ships, and as such, Captain Stronghold did his utmost to ensure his ship became the focal point for communication.

"Jennings, tell the *Vicksburg* to stand back and give us room to work. We don't want to be bunched too close together. Last thing I want is to sink them when I take this thing down," Stronghold ordered.

Stronghold was a hotshot captain who had a chip on his shoulder large enough to create a shadow. A military brat through and through, he was close to insufferable. His crew called him a tyrant, even if the true meaning of the word alluded to a callous, cutthroat individual, while most would argue that Stronghold lacked the fortitude for real violence.

Stronghold was dangerous. There was no other word to describe him. He did not appreciate the danger of the situation they were heading into. He did not care for tales of sea monsters. All he cared about was his reputation and making sure he climbed up the ladder. He had plans laid out to be the youngest everything right the way up to fleet admiral. Everything was structured, and he would stop at nothing to meet his targets. He had a lot of family watching him and some big shoes to fill. He was the youngest of five boys, all of them had joined the Navy, and he was already the best-ranked officer among them.

He was a ruthless man, an opportunist who had risen more on the mistakes of others than through his own merit. He had a knack of going through shit and coming out smelling like roses. His crew was all aware of this, none more so than his current in a long stream of XO's, Amanda Jennings. Three times now, she had been passed over for promotion as a result of her captain's failings. Twice he did not file the necessary paperwork through sheer spite that she had not taken the fall for an error in his judgement.

His crew functioned, but not from his command. Amanda ran the ship. Her interpretation of the captain's orders was what kept everything under control. She would regularly adjust the orders just enough to keep everything running smoothly.

***

Two miles to the east, the *Vicksburg* held their course and had their weapons systems online ready to engage anything that came their way. The boat placed the farthest to sea, they were the most likely to engage the creature, either directly or as a result of the submarines moves to drive the creature away from the coast.

The mission they had been given was split. The subs and the *Lassen* were there to drive the creature away from the shore, away from the civilians that were still crowding the beaches and the shallower waters. The cruisers were then there to do the heavy lifting and blow the monster out of the water. They were told to hold back and let the subs extend their lead to pick the creature off with the long-range weapons.

Captain John Holmes had also been given a very clear secondary objective, to keep his eyes on the *Gettysburg*. Stronghold's reputation went before him. He was considered a liability, and Captain Holmes had been tasked with ensuring he towed the line and did nothing that proved detrimental to the ship, its crew, or the mission as a whole. While not a fan of babysitting, Holmes understood the reasoning why he had been given the task. Men like Stronghold were dangerous, especially to those around them.

"Sir, we have received a message from the *Gettysburg*," Phillip Watson, the radioman, called out.

"I am not surprised by that at all. Just tell them we acknowledge. I have no desire to pick a fight with them while there is a bigger one out there," Holmes responded, turning his attention back to the sea.

He had been born and raised on the water. From water sports to daily swims in the ocean, year-round. He had been born with the sea in his blood. That was what his mother had said.

***

Over on the *Lassen*, the crew was quiet and getting on with their jobs. An experienced group of sailors, they worked the old ship with ease. Accustomed to its nuances and particular habits that could either be fought or adapted to.

Their captain was Lisa Morgan, a middle-aged woman who, while sociable, still believed in the strict gulf between a senior officer and her crew. A kind-hearted woman with intense hazel-coloured eyes that seemed the sparkle when she smiled, and darken to near black when mad. Her XO was Heather Watson, an intelligent lieutenant who herself stood on the brink of promotion. Although, Heather did not spend her time worrying over such things. What happened happened, and she would be grateful either way.

The Navy had saved her life. She had been a troublesome child, and as a young teen, she had been firmly set on the wrong path. A path that would have ended a long time ago, had she not changed her ways. Raised by her grandparents and pregnant at fourteen, she had not been a young lady that considered her choices. She lost the baby, and her grandfather had died just as she started to turn her life around. He had been her biggest supporter. Never once did he turn his back on her. He was always there for a shoulder to cry on. Oh, how she had cried. Unable to understand why she did the things she did, the battle within herself almost killed her. His death broken heart, and when the grief cleared, she was a much stronger person.

She had joined the Navy to honour her grandfather, and was happy to spend every day doing the job she loved. Promotions were nice, and she would never turn one down, but for her, working hard each day, remembering the man who had worked so hard to save her, was reward in itself.

The crew of the *Lassen* was ready to fight. They had all seen the news reports, and while they could not understand what happened, they accepted what they were up against. Determined to come out on top, everybody went about their job diligently and prepared to spring into action at the first sound of trouble.

RISE, KRAKEN!

CHAPTER 16

After witnessing the two helicopters get ripped apart, the gaggle of boats that had been heading out to sea could not turn around quick enough. The panic that spread through them caused havoc on the ocean. Boats moved in every which way, swerving around one another in order to be the first back to shore. Their voices hollered and roared as they cursed and threatened one another. Very few gave thought to the monster that lay beneath them. Only the quiet boats decided that a different course of retreat was needed and initially headed further out to sea so that they could cut around the masses and enjoy a near smooth and open run back to land.

They were the lucky ones.

Larry Jacobs was not one of those lucky, cool-headed individuals. Larry was an arrogant prick who was stuck in the middle of the chaos, cursing those before him for being idiots and those behind him for being morons. His voice was hoarse from the continuous verbal assault that he threw towards anybody that came within hearing distance.

In part, his readiness to curse at others over focusing on finding his own way through the mess, directly contributed to his downfall.

The water was choppy from the activity, which only meant that circular patch of millpond-flat water should have been spotted.

Beneath them, skulking on the ocean floor, lay a beast, injured and needing rest. The Kraken sought shelter in the only place possible: the seabed. Burrowing down, it dug and twisted its way to refuge.

On the surface, the patch of calm spread, and spread, growing to the size of a basketball, and then larger still to that of a car tyre. Only then did the centre start to sink, and the swirling vortex truly take form. Gentle at first, the boats passed by, oblivious. Larry Jacobs was different, his boat swerved around the others, moving too fast to be considered safe with everybody in such close proximity.

Proving or even speculating that his actions caused the vortex to sink and expand would be pointless, but just as his boat passed over the twisting patch of water, the ocean opened up and swallowed his boat. The rear of the craft sank backwards with such suddenness that Hank had no time to brace himself. He had no time to even consider his final words of thoughts. He had no time to even realize his end had come. He fell from the boat and landed in the water, caught by the pull of the vortex and dragged beneath the surface.

The boat stood vertically in the water for some time before disappearing, swallowed by the ever-growing swirling funnel. By that point, the fate of most of the boats in the close vicinity was sealed. The pool spread like a wildfire in the peak of summer, swallowing boats whole as it expanded, putting everything into its swirling maw.

The boats fell to the seabed where they met the beast that lay there. Angered by their intrusion on its rest, the Kraken rose once more.

The tentacles came from the sea, bursting upwards like projectiles. They grabbed at boats and flung them in every direction. People screamed as smaller limbs emerged, snaking around their bodies, hauling them into the air where they were held suspended, dangling above the vortex that now stretched to more than ten meters across.

The panic continued as boats collided under their own steam as people attempted to flee the beast they had all been so eager to see.

The water darkened, ink spread through the ocean, coating the boats and clinging to those that had fallen overboard and were swimming to their safety. The sickening sound of straining engines, screams of terror and the dull thud of bodies being crushed in the rush, rang out.

One man was whipped back and forth in a frenzy before being launched towards the shore. He flew over the boats and over the crowds, and crashed into the water like a meteor falling from space. His body tore apart on impact

The Kraken rose from the seabed, its gargantuan frame climbing to the surface, its outer beak already open, stretched wide to give room for its inner beak, its hungry, ink-spitting maw, to rise and issue a thunderous roar. The creature's cry thundered as if a hundred jets decided to take off on full thrust, the roar of a creature fiercer than the fires of hell releasing its rage upon the early.

The waters around the beast began to boil as its rage generated a blast of heat that flash-cooked the bodies in the water. Their skin reddening and blistering before they had the time to take but a few strokes.

The jaws slammed shut as the creature needed to protect itself from the surface air. Its outer shell was nothing more than a protective layer that allowed the beast to surface for short periods to feed, or the moments when its rage was too great to be contained.

The Kraken did not need its inner mouth to wreak destruction. Its real mouths were too numerous to count. Each suction cup on the underside of its limbs was hungry, each double set of pincer-like jaws could emerge from within its flesh and devour anything that came its way.

Blood filled the water as bodies were torn apart, and their flesh fed the beast and boats were swallowed by the ocean.

The carnage only ended when the first missile exploded against its shell and drove the monster below the surface. The blast disrupted the force of the vortex and calmed the waters. The Kraken sank beneath the waves, dragging down every living soul still caught in its grip.

The blast did nothing to damage the beast, but it understood what the attack signalled, and that was a fight the Kraken was not yet prepared for.

***

"Sir, we have a target on the creature," a voice called from behind the sonar unit on board the *Wyoming*.

The announcement brought both Captain Merriweather and his XO over to the station.

They studied the screen as the enormity of the Kraken was revealed.

"That thing is enormous," Lieutenant Young said, running through the mental calculation of size. The figures he got were too big to be believed.

'I'm afraid I have some bad news, sir, the game just changed," the same young technician spoke.

"How so?" the captain asked.

"How do I say this, the creature has engaged with the public. The boats are under attack."

Silence filled the bridge, and a few moments later, the sonar reading went crazy.

"What the hell was that?" Merriweather asked, his voice raised.

"I don't know, sir, something exploded, beneath the surface." The young technician swapped to a second console. "The seismic readings are also off the charts."

"What do we do, sir?" Young asked. "We can't risk any civilian casualties."

"I know. Bring us up to full speed. We need to get this creature's attention and lure her out to sea. Get a hold of the ships and tell them to spread into deeper water. We will drive this son of a bitch right to them." Merriweather moved back to the central position. He looked at the display screen.

"Sir," a second voice called out.

"What?" the captain asked, his eyes fixed on the zoomed-in image of the carnage in progress ahead of them.

"It's the *Alaska,* sir. She just fired her torpedoes," Lieutenant Young answered.

"What the hell does that arrogant son of a bitch think he is doing?" Merriweather thundered as the white streaks of the torpedoes moving through the water came into view. They sped through the water, spreading their trail like an infection spreading through a patient's veins. "He's going to get us all killed. Get him on the comms, I want to hear him explain himself."

***

"Are you seeing this, sir?" Lieutenant Regal asked as the creature rose from beneath the sea.

Captain Douglas had been glued to the periscope screen, ready and waiting to beat everybody else to the punch.

"I am indeed, Lieutenant," he answered, not once breaking his gaze on the unfolding scene. "Prepare to fire torpedoes."

The order was greeted with silence, the crew simply settling down to get the job done. There was no space for disagreement.

"Are you sure about this?" Regal asked, his potential resistance crumbling as soon as he caught the captain's glare.

"Our orders are to kill that beast. If none of the other ships are willing to make the first strike then we certainly will," Captain Douglas spoke, firm and resolute.

"Torpedoes are ready, sir," the quartermaster confirmed.

"Fire," the captain ordered without hesitation.

The sub rocked as the first torpedo launched.

"Watch and learn, Lieutenant, watch and learn," Douglas said with a smirk.

The call from the *Wyoming* came through almost to the second that Douglas had predicted in his head. He knew what was coming, and he knew exactly what he was going to say.

"Tell them to wait just one second," Douglas said, waving off the incoming call.

His eyes studied the screen where the body of the creature could be seen sitting on the water. They could see the attack that the civilian vessels were under, but the extent of the damage caused was hard to make out.

Captain Douglas counted down to himself, mouthing the words as he went to zero just as the explosion rocked the creature. He gave a cry of triumph as the fifteen-hundred-kilogram warhead struck its target and detonated with a ball of fire and steam. The vision was obscured momentarily, and when the smoke cleared, the creature could not be seen.

"Sonar?" The single word order was given and expected to be understood.

"Reports are clean, sir, there is nothing there," the sonar technician reported.

"Great news," Captain Douglas cried out, clapping his hands together as a smile spread across his face.

"But, sir, they did advise us that the creature could—" the technician began.

"I believe I will take the call from the *Wyoming* now." Douglas ignored the warning from his crew and continued on his own train of the thought.

"Don't worry yourself, Captain. We took care of the heavy lifting for you." Douglas could not help but sound high and mighty as he spoke.

"Just how fucking brainless are you?" The growl of Captain Merriweather roared through the speaker and successfully wiped the smug smile from Douglas's face.

"Captain Merri—"

"I don't want to hear any more of your bullshit, cock-waggling excuses. You just blew this entire thing. Not to mention the danger to civilians," Merriweather ranted, roaring into the speakers.

Standing nearby, Regal wondered how loud the captain's voice must be on the *Wyoming's* bridge.

"Captain, those people were under attack. My quick thinking probably saved their lives. You cannot deny that." Lance Douglas did not take kindly to being spoken down to, and having been caught off guard by the old man's response, he was all the more aggressive with his side of the conversation.

For a moment, no response came from the *Wyoming*, and the smirk returned to Douglas's lips.

"You broke the orders of this mission. The creature has retreated and we can no longer detect its presence. The one thing we had going in our favour is now gone as a result of your amateuristic, big headed, short-sighted idiocy." Merriweather showed no sign of stopping his verbal onslaught, and the crews on both bridges were beginning to feel awkward at being caught in the middle.

"Sir," voices echoed from both subs, and for the time being, the captains were broken apart and the argument set to one side. The communication lines closed, and both men returned to their attention to their own vessels.

"I have lost all trace of the creature, but I am picking up some strange seismic activity," the sonar operator on the *Wyoming* spoke up.

"Where?" the captains asked in tandem.

"Approximately three miles to the north." Both sonar operators gave the same location.

"What sort of activity?" Captain Merriweather asked, knowing that the same news was now being delivered to the crew of the *Alaska.*

"I don't know, sir. I would say an earthquake, but the readings are all wrong. An earthquake wouldn't be this slow." The young seaman looked up at his captain.

"Slow?"

"Yes, sir, the readings have returned to normal," the man spoke, shock and confusion heavy on his words.

"It must have been the creature, sir," Ian Young spoke up.

"If it is as large as we fear, and had a heavy exoskeleton, then that could be correct. It might be travelling low over the seabed." The sonar operator did not sound convinced, but then again, he had no other plausible explanation.

"Well, if that thing can take an MK-48 hit without issue, a strong exoskeleton makes sense," Captain Merriweather spoke, nodding as he did. He turned his attention back to the screen view of the horizon.

"Are we going to head out in pursuit, sir?" his XO asked.

"No, I want us to hold our course, keep moving along the coast. This bitch could still be lying inland. We already have the Vicksburg farther out, she can keep her eyes peeled on the deep water," Merriweather spoke. "Lieutenant Young, would you be as kind as to keep control over everything here. I need to go report back to the base and I want to have a chat with the other captains."

"Sir, yes, sir," Ian answered smartly.

He followed his captain towards the bridge's exit. "Are you really going to take action against Captain Douglas?" Ian asked, keeping his voice down low.

The captain turned and looked at his XO. He took a long steady breath and counted to ten before exhaling. "I don't think so. Not right now. Douglas is an ass, but he is a competent man. He just needed to learn a lesson in humility. However, I should not have to remind you, Lieutenant, that Captain Douglas is still a superior officer, so be mindful of your tone." Captain Merriweather gave a smile as he turned and walked away. "The bridge is yours until I return."

Captain Merriweather moved through to his wardroom. He settled, and after relaying the news through to the base, he called through to the other captains, noting the suddenly respectful voice of Captain Douglas as he gave his initial report on his decision to fire at the creature.

"Did you pick up that seismic anomaly a few moments ago?" Captain Morgan of the *Lassen* asked.

"Yes, we think the creature was dragging itself along the seabed," Merriweather answered.

"That was also the conclusion my sonar technicians have offered," Captain Douglas spoke up, all traces of his brash arrogance stripped from his words.

The conference was not video fed, so none of the other captains could see him, but Clarence still tried hard to keep the smile from his face. His hard-ass approach was something he seldom used, but whenever the need arose, the tactic never failed to be effective.

"Then we should head out deep and meet this thing head on," Captain Stronghold spoke up.

"I have to disagree you on that one. *Vicksburg*, you guys are already further out than the rest, keep on course and take a look. The rest of us, we need to continue in our current direction and make sure that creature is not returning to the shoreline," Merriweather instructed. Technically speaking, he was not the lead of the group, but his natural ability was to plan and lead.

"Sure thing, we will take a look and report back to the group. If we come into any trouble, we'll holler," Captain Holmes answered.

Merriweather liked Holmes. They had worked together plenty during their younger years of service. He respected the man, and understood that if anything happened, he could count on him to do the right thing. Not that he considered the others incapable, well, apart from Stronghold. That man was a first-class prick who rode his money and political leverage to get where he was. Morgan and even Douglas were different stories. Both were competent. Different in their styles, but effective none the less. However, they were from the generation after Holmes and himself. The two old timers understood that making the right decision may not always be the easy choice, or the one that makes the most sense at the time of making.

Everything in life was a chess game, and you needed to be one step ahead. The younger captains, well, they tried, but rather than chess, all the academy taught was checkers. One dimensional always push forward tactics that could, and often did work. However, sometimes they were not necessarily the best approach.

Nobody had much else to add, and so after a round of discussions on what they had seen and how they planned to deal with the creature once they had it in position, the captains ended the communication.

Clarence Merriweather sat in the wardroom for a while. He mulled over everything that had happened thus far and played around with the different thoughts running through his head.

If the creature had an outer shell that could take a direct torpedo strike, then the plan to simply blast the thing out of the water was not necessarily as easy of a task as people first anticipated.

Injuring the creature was not a problem. The limbs were soft, so that at least gave them a place to strike, but to take the creature down was going to take something special. He just had no idea what. Being a man not given to panicked reactions, Merriweather decided to wait it out a little longer. Time had proven that solutions would present themselves. The first order of business remained the same, to force the thing out to sea. Keeping the civilians safe was always key, especially with the weapons they were planning on unleashing on the beast.

Moving back to the bridge, the captain entered but said nothing. He stood back a moment, admiring how his XO moved from station to station, communicating, checking and cross-checking everything that came his way. He smiled to himself. He found comfort in the knowledge that his ship was in such good control. Ian, while still young, but held a lot of potential, more than any of the others in their group. He was a little over enthusiastic at times, and would on occasion overthink things, but never with anything but the best of intentions. Clarence was certain that he would make a grand captain, and not in the too distant future either.

"Sir." Ian turned around and looked at Clarence.

"What is it, Lieutenant?" Clarence asked, pushing his XO just a little bit.

"Sir, we are getting some strange readings not far from where that seismic anomaly was reported."

"What sort of readings?" Clarence asked as he strode into the centre of the bridge.

"Multiple targets. I count five, sir. They seem to be moving out into deeper water," the sonar technician reported.

"How large?" Captain Merriweather was already running through possible explanations.

"Smaller than the creature, sir, but they are definitely organic, and solid masses." The news was troubling, and certainly not something any of them had anticipated.

"The creature is our number one priority. We should stay on the mission," Captain Merriweather decided, trusting his instincts. "I need a comms link through the *Lassen*."

"Captain Merriweather," the softly spoken yet authoritative of Lisa Morgan spoke first. "I was expecting your call."

"I am sure you were, Captain Morgan." Clarence smiled. "I assume I do not need to mention the foreign objects picked up on the sonar?"

"You do not, I have already told my pilots to ready themselves." Lisa Morgan was no fool, but being a woman in the military, she had always felt the need to force herself to stay ahead of the game. She liked Clarence Merriweather. He had never been anything other than courteous to her, and she had the pleasure of spending several years as his XO on an old destroyer, but that did not allow her to play favourites.

"I never doubted you," Captain Merriweather answered. "Then I guess everything is under control. Please let us know what your pilot reports. Those objects are certainly troubling."

"Roger that, Captain," Lisa answered before closing the channel.

***

Enzo Rowan received his orders and was pleased to be able to get off the boat and up into the air. The one place in the world where he always felt comfortable.

His SeaHawk sat on deck ready to go as he emerged. His co-pilot, Freddie Moore, was out sick. He had suffered a sudden appendicitis just the day before and was currently recovering from surgery.

Enzo did not mind, however; he had flown solo before, and a simple recon flight would not be difficult. The extra pair of eyes always helped, but he was not going to going to make a fuss.

The weather was beautiful and the visibility perfect. He could see his targets not long after he took off from the deck.

He could see the five shadows spreading through the water. But what held his attention even more was the spreading pool of black that stretched several hundred meters in diameter and matched the location he had been given as a secondary target.

"Captain, I've got something strange out here," Enzo called back to the boat.

"What is it, Lieutenant?" the *Lassen* responded.

"I have visuals on the targets, but there is something else. I'm over the location of the anomaly, and well, I've got something that looks like we have an oil slick spreading out here. Are there any reports of a ruptured line in the area?" Enzo spun his bird around to get a full look at the spill.

"Negative, Lieutenant. I don't have any reports coming through, but that doesn't mean the creature hasn't ruptured something. I will make sure it gets reported," the *Lassen*'s communication officer replied.

"Roger that, Lassen," Enzo answered. "Wait, I see something else. I don't have clear visuals, but something is floating on the surface the middle of the slick. We need to get somebody out here to take a look, this looks bad."

"Noted, Lieutenant, continue to the primary targets. We need to know what we are up against," the *Lassen* replied.

Enzo climbed once more and headed out after the others. The shadows had spread out, and several had sunk deeper in the ocean and were almost disappeared from view.

Swooping in, Enzo tensed as the creature broke the surface for a second. From distance, the thing looked like a spider, or at least that was the closest living creature Enzo could think of to associate the beasts with. They had a bulky body that seemed to have a pointed head and a wider, rounded rear. Eight joined legs sprang from its body, four on each side. They were thrusting the creature through the water in a digging motion, scooping its body along.

The body only surfaced for a brief moment, and then disappeared from view, shooting beneath the water with a speed that bordered on instantaneous.

"*Lassen,* we have bogeys in the water. I don't know what the hell they are, but I don't think we want to find out either. I've never seen anything like them," Enzo reported back to his ship.

"Roger that, come on home, Lieutenant, we will have a full debrief when you land," the voice of the communications officer came through.

Enzo turned his back on the creatures, which had all disappeared from view, and headed back to the boats. He could make out the submarines to his left, their direction changing to bring them out towards the strange oily mass. Further behind them, the ships headed his way. Their bearings also adjusted to bring them out into deeper waters.

He had no idea what the beasts were, and while he held no desire to meet the creatures again, he accepted that avoiding them was an impossibility. Suddenly, the idea of staying in the air became even more appealing, but he could not hide in the sky forever.

Both the captain and her XO stood waiting for him on the deck, and were by the side of the chopper before the rotors powered down. Enzo sat for a moment, waiting and gathering his thoughts. He was certain of what he had seen, but putting that sight into words, convincing words at that, would be no easy task.

"What did you see out there?" Captain Morgan asked before Enzo had both feet on the deck. She had no plans to wait until they could move inside before the debriefing began.

"I don't know what they were," Enzo answered honestly.

"Then describe them to me," Lisa Morgan said. She spoke softly; she understood the strange nature of their foe, and was willing to suspend any and all belief.

"I guess giant spiders. They had enough legs, and large black bodies. They swam through the water and disappeared. One surfaced for a second but not long enough for me to learn anything. All I know is that they are bad news, and we have something else to worry about."

"Walk with me, Lieutenant," the captain spoke to Enzo. "Lieutenant Watson, you have control of the bridge. Hold our current course until I return. Should we come across anything out there while I am gone, you have my complete authority to act accordingly."

"Yes, sir," Heather Watson answered, and turn to leave the *Lassen's* deck.

Enzo followed Captain Morgan as she led him through the corridors of the ship up to the combat information centre where the other captains were already waiting for his report. Enzo had stood before a large group of senior officers, but he had never felt so nervous doing so. His heart pounded in his chest, because while everybody in their small attack ground was up to speed on what they were facing, standing up and describing a spider-like sea creature the size of an elephant still seemed plain ridiculous.

The meeting was done and dusted in a flash. They asked Enzo for his report, he ran through everything swiftly and as concisely as he could. They excused almost immediately, to Enzo's visible relief.

He headed straight back to his bunk to get some sleep. He had an idea that he would be back in the air before too long, and wanted to make sure he remained as fresh as possible.

CHAPTER 17

Luke Stronghold sat in his comms room with his hands behind his head. He leaned back in the chair and looked for all intents and purposes like a man who had not a care in the world.

He looked around and nodded in the right places. When called upon, he voiced his agreement, knowing full well that voicing any form of disagreement with the orders of old man Merriweather would serve no purpose. The old captain was set in his ways and would shut down anything that he thought was disobedience. Merriweather was just like Captain Holmes. They were old dogs, relics that came from an older time, a defunct school of thought that was weighted unfairly against free thinkers. Visionary was a strong term, and not one Stronghold would use through choice, yet when comparing his mind-set against the other captains in their group, he could not think of a more fitting word. Risk versus reward was too radical a concept for the old men to understand or even contemplate. For Stronghold, however, that was what he lived for. The reward, the risk … the thrill of the game.

"XO Jennings, I believe the time has come for us to change our course." He smiled smugly. "I want us to cut behind the *Vicksburg* and head out into open waters."

"Sir, do you think that—?"

"Yes, I do think so. I am the captain of this ship, and you, Amanda, are lucky to be on board today. For today is the day that the *Gettysburg* makes its name." Luke paid attention to the way his XO winced at his usage of her full first name. "I am tired of playing along with their outdated way of thinking. The future is now. We are bold, and we are brave. This is our chance to make a stand. Stand with me and we will conquer these creatures, win this conflict, and when we return to port, the rewards will be there for us to claim."

He got up from the table and left without saying another word. He didn't need to say anything. Amanda was used to the way he gave an order only to retreat back to his quarters, leaving her the task of informing the crew. The annoyance this time being they were working over short distances and specific targets. Tweaking the orders to redirect the ship in a better, more acceptable fashion without her captain noticing would be impossible. She also knew that he would have no problem reporting her for insubordination. He had tried twice before, but each time he had let the matter settle before they reached land again.

With a sigh, Amanda rose from the table, readjusted her uniform, and made her way to the bridge.

***

"Sir, it's the *Gettysburg,*" the voice called out through the intercom directly into the communications room where Captain Holmes sat in conversation with the captain of the *Wyoming.*

"What about the *Gettysburg?* What has Stronghold done now?" Forster asked. He had been expecting the cocky captain to say or do something stupid. He had been far too quiet during both of their recent group calls.

"Well, they have altered their course. They are setting up to pass behind us, sir," the technician on the other end of the line spoke. "We tried to raise them, but we got no answer on either of the frequencies."

"God dammit, that son of a bitch is going to get himself killed," Holmes roared, slamming his hands on the table.

Holmes moved from the comms room through to the combat centre where he tried to get some recognition from the *Gettysburg* but failed in every attempt.

"They have moved behind us, sir. What would you suggest?" Lieutenant Forster asked, looking to his captain for advice.

Captain Holmes did the thing he was trained to do. He made a decision. The only one that really could be made. He broke formation and moved after the *Gettysburg*, doing so only after pointing out the foolishness of Stronghold's actions. Both Morgan and Merriweather agreed with the decision, while Captain Douglas had at first voiced his support for the *Gettysburg's* actions, only to later change his mind.

Good sense prevailed, and everybody agreed the *Vicksburg* would follow her sister ship and try to communicate with them and convince Stronghold to re-join the formation.

With two of their numbers depleted, the subs decided to pull back a little and close in on the *Lassen*. This move produced another shift in the formation when the *Alaska* feinted to pull back and actually turned and ended up ahead of the *Wyoming*. The move was a cheap shot and annoyed Merriweather no end, but he also had faith that having heard the anger in the discussion relating to Stronghold's decision, Douglas would not be so stupid as to try something similar.

***

Stronghold had a smile from ear to ear as his ship passed behind its sister. The thrill of the open sea lay ahead of him, and he could hear glory beckoning him. They were destined to make history. Everything was there, the monster, the old dogs, and the single young gun. Now was his chance to strike.

"I want to all six guns brought ready. I have a feeling we will be coming across something soon," he spoke to his crew.

"Sir, the *Vicksburg* are trying to contact us on the internal communication channel," his XO spoke, whispering so as not to cause any alarm at their captain's rogue antics. "I really think you should take the call, sir."

"That is why I am the captain of this ship, Amanda. You feel guilty for having taken a decision. You let their misguided judgement cloud your own. We will ignore the old man until he is calling to congratulate us." The arrogance wafted from Stronghold's persona like a bad cologne.

"Sir, we have something on the sonar. It's coming in fast, five hundred yards and closing," the sonar operator's voice called out, cutting through the tension that had developed between the two senior officers.

"How did you let them get that close?" Stronghold growled, caught off guard for a moment. "Get those guns smoking, now!"

A few moments later, the two .50 calibre machine guns began to roar, firing at the black-bodied creature that charged towards them. Not slowed by the lead barrage, the creature sank beneath the surface.

"It's too close sir, it's moving beneath us," a panic-filled voice replied.

Everybody felt the boat shudder as the creature impacted with the craft's hull. The bridge rumbled, but Stronghold could only laugh.

"Those things can't hurt us," the captain proclaimed, making sure that everybody heard. "I want full speed, let's move past this thing and send one of the big fish after the fucker. I want a torpedo ready to hit the water the second we have daylight between us and this thing." Stronghold could taste victory and could practically hear them cheering his name.

"Sir, we can't get loose. This thing won't let go," a report came back from the sonar room

"We have reports of a hull breach, sir," Amanda spoke as she moved across the bridge to stand face to face with her commanding officer. "That thing has clamped onto the hull and is trying to break its way in."

"Nonsense. I want full power on the port engines, cut power to starboard. We will shake this son of a bitch loose." The order was given and with a sudden lurch, the *Gettysburg* turned sharply in the water.

"Torpedoes are ready, sir," the weapons officer reported.

"Sir, the target is free, but we have two more coming in, heading for the *Vicksburg*." Suddenly, the combat centre came alive with chatter.

"Fire the torpedoes. The *Vicksburg* is a big girl, she can look after herself. They came after us because they wanted to play with the big boys, well now here is their chance."

The boat shuddered once again as the front-mounted launch tubes sent an mk-50 shooting into the water.

The warhead locked onto its target, and within a few seconds, a thunderous explosion rolled through the air like thunder as the warhead detonated. Captain Stronghold and his crew cheered as the black body transformed into a floating ball of flame. Blood and flesh flew in every direction, legs blasted across all points of the compass.

"Target has been neutralized, sir." A raucous round of cheers rolled through the ship, to which Captain Stronghold stood to claim his plaudits. Amanda stood in the corner of the command centre, watching as the two new creatures closed in and onto the *Vicksburg*.

By the time his XO had managed to gain his attention, they were too far from the Vicksburg to do anything but sit back and watch their destruction.

CHAPTER 18

Forrest and this two new friends were surprisingly given free range over the base, well, to all areas Captain McCall deemed suitable. Randolph had insisted that both Pete and Forrest be treated as if they were captains, and allowed to eat in the officer's hall and enjoy other such on-site perks.

Captain McCall agreed, and once the boats left the harbour and on their way to engage the creature, his disposition changed.

The three men sat eating a meal when a young, crisp-looking soldier approached McCall and spoke to him in hushed tones, eyeing up the three civilians that sat with him. The three men sat in silence as McCall laid down his fork, wiped his mouth and stood from the table. All the while, the blood seemed to be draining from his face.

"Thank you, you may go now," McCall said to the man, who turned and left without uttering a word.

The military way fascinated Forrest. The dedication to subservience was something he could never get his head around.

"What happened?" Randolph asked.

"Not here. Come with me." McCall turned and walked out of the mess hall before the others could so much as lay their cutlery down. They scurried after him and out into the open air.

Until then, they had moved everywhere in a car, or worst case, a weird sort of golf cart, but now that they were on foot, the heat of the Florida sun and the size of the base had them all sweating by the time they caught up to the striding general.

"What's happened?" Randolph asked, his powerful stride matching and out-pacing that of McCall.

Randolph moved his body around to face McCall and brought him to a stop.

"There are more of them out there. They have attached the *Vicksburg* and the *Gettysburg*. We need to get to the control centre now," McCall answered, and Randolph nodded, moving to one side.

The group of four men crossed the complex and entered the command centre without question. Everybody they walked passed on their way stopped and saluted all four men, even if there were some curious gazes being cast towards Forrest.

Inside, the centre was a buzz of activity. There were computer consoles and screens showing all manner of information. Too much to be taken in or understood by just one brain. They were quickly led into a meeting room on the far right of the room

"We got reports from a recon flight that there are more creatures in the sea. These things are … well, just take a look at the video from the flight." They turned their attention towards a large monitor.

They stared at the screen as the video, recorded from a camera in the nose of Enzo's Seahawk, came into focus. They leaned in close to study the spreading oil slick and the strange mass floating in the center. The helicopter turned in a slightly nauseating piece of camerawork. The change in angle caught the creature that surfaced just before it disappeared, its multiple legs pulling its body through the water.

They replayed the tape three times, stopping on the best available image of the creature.

"What the fuck is that? Have you come across this in your research before?" McCall asked, turning to face Forrest.

"Me, no, I've never seen … one second, bring the video back around. Back to the start, to that shot of the black slick," Forrest asked.

The video was refreshed, and the young seaman who had been put in charge of the tech for their meeting paused the film when Forrest asked.

"There, in the middle. What is that?" Forrest got up and pointed to the screen.

"Looks like oil to me," Pete answered. Out of the three of them, he looked the worst for wear. The sudden sobriety clearly weighed heavy in his gut.

"It does, but I don't think that is what this is. We heard the pilot ask about ruptured oil lines, because of some anomaly." Forrest did not turn around to further articulate his words.

"Yes, all of the ships picked up some strange seismic readings. They reasoned that creature was scraping the seabed. We assume as a result of the torpedo strike," McCall answered, moving up to stand beside Forrest. He could sense that the old man was thinking of something, and that put him in control.

"I would agree with you, but looking at this, I don't think the creature was injured. Not in the way you are hoping. You see that there." Forrest pointed at the organic mass that was floating on the surface.

"Yes."

"That is a sack, like an egg sack. That black is not oil from a ruptured line, but ink. That creature we are hunting was pregnant, and those things in the water, are her young."

For a second, nobody in the room spoke. Silence reigned as they allowed the thoughts to move through their minds.

"But how? She has been underground since the eighties," Pete finally spoke. "I know because I put her there."

"I don't think you did. I think you killed her mate," Forrest returned.

"Her mate?"

"Yes, think about it. If there is one, then there had to be at least one other to create this one, and something tells me these things are not breeding asexually. I think you killed her mate, and this thing has been gestating ever since." Forrest turned to look at the group.

"Well, pregnant or not, one or two of them, I don't really care," McCall began. "All this means is we have more targets to attack."

"Yes, that is true, Captain, but have you ever come across a mother that was not protective of her young?" Forrest spoke.

The statement brought silence to the meeting room. Forrest didn't need to offer any further explanation. Not that there was time, for a few seconds after he spoke, the door to the meeting room opened and a sickly, pale-looking recruit stumbled inside.

"Sir, the …"

CHAPTER 19

Captain Holmes was focused on catching up to the *Gettysburg* and had actually envisioned his fist connecting with Stronghold's jaw. In his mind, he even imagined two teeth come hurling from the mouth as the cocksure captain hit the deck.

His sonar technicians provided a constant run down on the targets moving towards the *Gettysburg*. The two creatures that attacked them came from nowhere. They appeared without warning. One minute the water was clear, the next they were under attack. The creatures moved like aquatic ghosts.

"The *Gettysburg* has fired a torpedo, sir." The notification came just moments before the confirming explosion. The sound of the explosion and the subs close proximity to the blast allowed for the other creatures to latch onto the *Vicksburg* hull. Their limbs clamped down hard, their weight pushing the vessel off centre, dragging its starboard side down towards the water.

"I want everybody armed and on deck, ready to fight. Swing the front gun around and see if we can't pick them off as they come over the side." Captain Holmes gave the orders, keeping his calm as best he could in the process. Panic would never turn the tide of the confrontation in their favour.

The sound of the heavy limbs clanging and banging as the creatures climbed on board the *Vicksburg* echoed through every level of the craft. Those that had not been on the bridge had no clue what awaited them, and as they crew lined the deck, weapons ready, they came face to face with a beast no training on earth could prepare them for.

The thick back shell emerged over the top of the railing, and the group opened fire. There were two groups of half a dozen that had formed on the deck; an official welcoming committee for the creatures.

The air filled with the sound of automatic fire. The cacophonous roar was an impressive sound, and the lead rained down on the creatures was fierce, yet all efforts were in vain. The creature's outer skeleton ate the onslaught and merely threw the bullets straight back at those that fired them. Two men went down, their hands grasping at their throats as blood spurted between their fingers and over the deck.

"Fall back." Petty Officer Nathan Hawk gave the order as he and the three remaining members of his team yielded ground to the creatures. "Stinger, you're the best shot here. When they come over the railing, I want you to put some hot lead in their belly."

"Roger that, sir," Stinger answered, dropping to one knee and bringing his rifle to his shoulder.

"You sure this is going to work?" Burt Horowitz asked.

"No, but most creatures are soft in the belly," Hawk answered.

The wait did not last long. Stingers drowned out the noise, his eyes focused on the spot he wanted to place the first bullet. The time came and he fired without thinking. Half a dozen shots rang out and sunk into the creature's soft underbelly. The thing shuddered and gave a childlike shriek as black blood oozed from the wounds.

Stinger fired another burst but the creature hauled its body over the railings and onto the deck. Its body sat down low, blood leaking around the edges, but for the most part being contained beneath its bulk.

"What the hell? These things ain't got no eyes," Reg Fowler spoke. He took a step closer to the thing. "I think it's dead," he said, turning his head to look at Hawk but his world went suddenly askew.

The tentacle had shot out from beneath the creature like a whip and sliced through skin and bone with ease. Hot pain flashed through Reg's mind before his head fell to the deck. Somehow, his body remained standing.

The group opened fire, but achieved nothing.

The creature's legs extended from its body like poles before bending at odd angles to propel its bulk from the floor. A set of wet, scorpion-like pincers unfurled from the pointed tip as the creature began to make its way across the bridge. Behind them, the second attack group was losing their battle. Four of their members already lay dead on the deck, blood and body parts scattered over the ship.

The creatures rose to give their body a good three feet of ground clearance. Small, underdeveloped tentacles dangled from their undercarriage.

Nathan backed his men up once again as the creature advanced, and they found themselves with their backs against the railings. They looked around just as the final two members of the other group were torn apart by the other creature's mandible claws. They snipped the bodies clean in half. The two men both managed to fire into the limb's meat as they fell in a splatter of purple sausage-like intestines and other organs. The creature shrank back from the onslaught, one pincer hanging down, dragging against the deck.

"Grenade, grenade." The call went out, and the remaining three men threw themselves to the floor. A few moments later, consecutive explosions tore across the *Vicksburg's* deck.

Lieutenant Forster looked down from the upper deck as the battle unfolded. The groups did not stand a chance against the two creatures. Lining up his sights, a grenade in each hand, he waited for the right moment to launch his own strike. His aim was true and the grenades rolled beneath the creature's bellies just as they exploded. The ship was blown to shit as the explosions tore through the creatures, blew apart their shells from the inside out, and tore through the metal of the ship's deck and lower-level walls.

Alarms and klaxons sounded, and when the smoke cleared, the extent of the damage became clear. Two gaping holes in the deck revealed the lower floor, while smouldering chunks of sea monster meat littered the deck.

The lieutenant searched the deck, his eyes looking for the true ramifications of the damage, as well for the men who had been on the deck with the monsters. His eyes found the men. They were slowly staggering to their feet, their bodies plastered with blood and guts. The insides of the creatures appeared to have a strange, web-like consistency.

Frasier moved to head back to the bridge, eager to hear from those below deck about the health of the ship. Their involvement in the conflict may well be over, but they had left their mark. At best, they would limp back to port. At worst, they would have to shuffle over to one of the other ships and sacrifice the *Vicksburg* to the sea.

He didn't get far. His legs gave out beneath him, and he fell to the deck, landing with a wet splat. Blood pooled around him. Frasier brought his hands to his belly, his trembling fingers touching the large shard of torn iron that protruded from his gut. The gash stretched across his belly and spilled blood in a torrent, pulling with it strings of intestines, despite the twisted shard of metal blocking the wound.

He heard the ship groan as the engines powered up, but it was too late for him.

CHAPTER 20

"Sir, the *Gettysburg* and *Vicksburg* are under attack," Ian Young relayed the news to his CO, and stood back as the man's face darkened with rage.

"That idiot," he growled. "Put me through to the *Lassen* and the *Alaska.*"

The call was a simple one, and neither of the opposing captains offered any argument. The *Alaska* would lead the *Lassen* along the coast to investigate the ink spillage. The reports from Mayport confirmed the creature had given birth to the things that were attacking the other boats. Discussions came to the reasoning that having just given birth, the monster would be in a weakened state, meaning the ideal time to strike had come.

The *Wyoming* headed after the *Gettysburg* and her sister, and they would sweep back in land in an attempt to converge on the Kraken, wherever it was hiding.

However, the best laid plans are often those that go the most awry, as the *Wyoming* was about to notice.

"Sir, we have something incoming," the radar technician called out, his voice panicked.

"Is it the creature?" Merriweather asked. He was uptight and ready for a fight. Stronghold had gotten under his skin, and as a result, people were most likely going to die.

"No sir, this is … airborne." A few seconds later, the sky darkened for a brief second as the sun was eclipsed. The shadow passed before most people realized anything had even occurred, but the resulting crash and the wall of water that rolled their way got their attention. The wave impacted the side of the *Wyoming*, sending everybody on board flying. Alarms sounded as computers shorted out from the aggressive jolt.

"I need a report. What the hell as that, and who fired at us?" Merriweather called as he hauled himself to his feet. He was unhurt, but the same could not be said for the rest of the folk on the bridge.

Several were bloodied and battered, but as far as he could tell, they were all in one piece.

"Sir, I believe that was the creature, sir … the Kraken," the voice stuttered.

"Are you telling me that thing can fucking fly?" Merriweather roared, his patience worn thin and his anger for Stronghold boiling over in a way that it had not done since his youth.

"Negative, sir. I mean the Kraken launched the projectile, which … well, I believe it was the *Vicksburg*, sir … her stern at least."

"Get me visuals, now, and take us below the surface." Merriweather reacted in an instant, his need for a fight clouding his judgement for a moment. Losing visuals as they dove was a risk, but one Merriweather was prepared to take, for his ship was better under the water than on the surface

The main screen sprang to life and the entire bridge fell silent. From captain down through the ranks, everybody held their breath and simply stared at the creature that rose before them. Even the *Wyoming* herself seemed to cease her rattles and shudders in order to truly take in the sight before them.

The Kraken had risen to the surface, its entire body, or so Merriweather hoped. At least a dozen large arms pierced the water and wafted far above the beasts head. One such tentacle was wrapped around the rear half of the *Vicksburg*. He swayed to and fro as it holding nothing. The large bulbous head of the creature had extended from the opened-up outer shell. The Kraken's body continued to grow, rollout outwards from within the shell, effectively turning itself inside out, or maybe outside in, given that what emerged could only be considered the creature's true face.

Eyes that burned orange like the fires of hell glared at the ocean. The hungry maw that was the creature's mouth unfurled, pulling back in four enormous folds, bloomed like a paper flower revealing row after row of spiny teeth.

"Good God in heaven," Captain Merriweather said, not caring if his crew heard the fear in his voice.

"I don't think God, or heaven for that matter, had any part in this things creation," Rajesh Sign, the quartermaster said, moving beside the captain to stare at the screen.

"Sir, look, the *Gettysburg*," the XO called, pointing through the forest of tentacles to where the cruiser could be made out through the gap in the flailing flesh.

"Prepare the torpedoes. I want two fish in the water, now!" Captain Merriweather ordered, his voice booming. The time for games had passed. They had one shot to save themselves, and if they were lucky, a threesome with twins lucky, maybe the *Gettysburg* also.

The torpedoes were fired and the submarine sank deeper beneath the waves.

"Sir, we have one of those things incoming, one thousand yards and closing," a voice called over the speakers.

"Fire aft torpedoes," Merriweather roared as the Kraken launched what remained of the *Vicksburg* deep into the ocean.

Water bloomed behind the beast, as the *Lassen* opened fire. From what Merriweather could make out, before his own two fish hit the mark, the cruiser had fired three blasts in quick succession. One hit the body and two seemed to damage some of the larger tentacles. They disappeared into the water, withdrawing from the shock of the blast.

The creature's mouth opened even further and a roar was produced that made the *Wyoming* shake, hitting them like a depth charge.

Another explosion nearby signified the end of the third kraken baby, but nobody took the time celebrate the victory.

When the smoke cleared, and the result of the torpedo strikes became clear, the body of the beast was slipping beneath the waves, black blood spurting from its broken body, clouding the water.

"Direct hit, sir. We have the creature on the run. The *Lassen* just confirmed, the target is heading out to sea," the sonar technician called out.

This news did generate a gentle murmur of congratulations, but everybody understood one fight did not make a war.

"We have her on the run. Lieutenant, call in the other ships, and get me in touch with Mayport. We are going to chase this bitch down and make her pay what she did to the *Vicksburg*."

CHAPTER 21

"Gentlemen, come with me," Captain McCall addressed his three guests. They left the meeting room and were surprised to see both the master chief and Lieutenant Harrington waiting for them. "Follow them, they will take you where you need to go."

Nobody spoke, there was no need. They all had an idea of what was going down. However, the reality could not have been further from what was on their minds. While they were being escorted off the base, there was no dark-windowed car waiting for them, but rather a warmed-up SeaHawk. The pilot smiled at them as they approached him.

"Gonna be a cosy ride, ladies and gentlemen," Enzo offered with a smile.

"Story of my life," Master Chief Elmers answered immediately.

"Oh OK, straight talking kind of guy. I respect that," Enzo said with a lot less enthusiasm that the words would proclaim. "Step right in and we will be off."

"Where are we going?" Forrest asked.

"My orders are to bring you all to the *Lassen.* What happens after that, well, it's up to the captain … captains," Enzo corrected when his eyes fell on Randolph uniform. "Pleasure seeing you again, Captain Wiseman. I served with you way back when, on the *Arleigh-Burke.*"

Randolph nodded his head and offered a smile. Truth was he did recognize the pilot, but his mind was preoccupied with a myriad of other thoughts.

They loaded into the chopper and were airborne in a matter of minutes.

"Why are they bringing us to the ship?" Forest asked. He was not adverse to some adventure, but he did not appreciate being led blindly into a warzone.

"I believe they need your expertise on this creature," Enzo answered from the chopper's cockpit. "Can't say any more than that, sir, because, well, because I just don't know." He laughed and pulled his machine into a swinging turn that brought them ahead of the ship landing on the deck into the wind.

They were met on the deck by Captain Morgan and her XO. They exchanged pleasantries and were then hurried off the deck. Enzo's chopper was quickly pushed to one side to make way for another.

"You guys are right on time," Captain Morgan called above the noise of the approaching Seahawk.

"Are we having a party?" Randolph asked.

"Something like that. Captain Merriweather of the *Wyoming* wanted to have a meeting with us all. In light of losing the *Vicksburg*."

The group stood and waited as the chopper landed. A young captain got out and walked over to them. He smiled and shook hands with everybody. He stood tall and straight, he had a cockiness to him that was off-putting at first sight, but after a few minutes of being in his presence, they all understood the brashness was just his natural character.

The SeaHawk left and quickly returned with a rather smug-looking Captain Stronghold. Randolph and the Forrest took an immediate dislike to the man. While Douglas was cocky, this man was clearly just a cock. Everything from his smile and his walk to the way he wore his uniform screamed first-class cunt.

The helicopter returned a third time, and an older man jumped out. He ignored everybody that stood near him and made a direct and fast-paced line for the gathered group. He walked like a man on a mission, his face a thundercloud of rage. His fists were white-knuckled balls at his sides.

Captain Merriweather had decided his course of action the moment he demanded the meeting on board the *Lassen*. He strode up to Stronghold grabbed the man by the shoulder, spinning him around. The right hook was thrown with a power that even Merriweather did not realize he possessed. Much like in his mind, Stronghold crumbled, his legs went out from under him and his head snapped back. Blood flowed from his split upper lip and injured nose. He hit the deck in a heap, not moving.

"Alright, I'm done. Thank you for having us, Captain." He smiled at Captain Morgan and nodded at the others. As he strode away, something caught his eye, a bloody tooth lay on the *Lassen's* deck. The old captain smiled.

Clarence Merriweather climbed back into the waiting helicopter and left immediately. Leaving the stunned party behind, and an unconscious Luke Stronghold on the floor.

"What was that about?" Forrest felt compelled to ask.

"That is what happens to trust fund babies when they realize this is life, not a fucking game," Lisa Morgan growled, turning to leave Stronghold on his knees on the deck. "I believe that is all, Captain Stronghold. You may also return to your vessel, Captain Douglas. I think we all know what we have to do."

The four remaining vessels were soon cutting through the water, in a new formation. The *Wyoming* had taken the lead once more, with the *Lassen* close behind. The *Gettysburg* trudged behind them, gliding silently through the water, while the *Alaska* brought up the rear. They were spread in a rough diamond formation.

The first of the Kraken young attacked the *Lassen*, moving up from beneath, surging from the seabed. The submarines picked up on the attack, however, and with the *Lassen* pulling out a tight-neck evasive manoeuver, the *Wyoming* was able to take the thing out with a close-range torpedo strike.

"That's at least three down. These things are just fodder. We need to find the mother. The ink trail dried up, but we had her rocked with those strikes," Merriweather spoke once the group had reformed.

"Captain Merriweather, this is Forrest Jones. I think I know where the creature is heading," Forrest replied, using the private communication channel to talk directly to the *Wyoming*.

"I am all ears, Mr. Jones," the *Wyoming's* captain answered.

"There are lots of small islands around here, are there not?"

"Yes, there are plenty," Clarence answered. He understood what the man was suggesting, but would not steal the man's thunder.

"If we have this creature injured, as you suggest, then the logical move, for any animal, would be to seek shelter, most likely by one of the islands, in the shallows."

"What makes you think that?" Merriweather asked.

"Just a hunch. I have been hunting this creature for some time, and every time I have been close, I was either on land or in shallow water. She needs to recover from the damage you did, and from giving birth. Survival is her primary goal now." Forrest had their attention. He took over the communication, and the depleted attack group listened to his advice without question.

"Sir, we have an island approximately seventeen miles to the east. It's in friendly waters too," Ian Young spoke up, pointing out the island on an electronic map that appeared on the bridge's main screen.

"Very good, Lieutenant. Change our course and inform the others. I want us to head in first, and the *Alaska* to follow. Tell the surface vessels to hold back. I want them in range for a missile strike if needed. No point in using them for small arms fire." As Merriweather spoke, an explosion rumbled through the water a mile to the rear.

"One more down, sir," the voice of XO Jennings called. After the incident with Stronghold, the other captains handed temporary control of the ship over to Amanda, even if Stronghold was still to be considered its captain.

"Very good, Jennings," Captain Merriweather replied, before going on to explain his plan to the young officer.

With everybody on the same page, the subs moved away to the island, and the confrontation that awaited them.

With the loss of the *Vicksburg* still fresh in their minds, and news of their captain's assault on Captain Douglas rife among the men on all ships, a tense atmosphere ran through both subs.

CHAPTER 22

Captain Merriweather took his sub to the small island while the Alaska held back. The small patch of land certainly could not contain any inhabitants, human inhabitants at least. The entire landmass comprised of a tall rock with some greenery around the base.

"Sir, readings are placing a geothermal core in the middle of the island, but other than that, we are reading nothing," Ian Young fed back the findings to his captain.

"Any signs of the creature?" Clarence asked.

"No, sir. There is nothing to indicate it came—"

The submarine shook as something crashed against it.

"It's one of the other ones, sir," a voice called through the intercom. "It's clamped on hard."

A sudden hush ran through the vessel. The quiet ensuring everybody heard the crunch as a leg shot through the *Wyoming's* hull. Alarms sounded as water began to fill the craft.

"Take us to the surface!" Clarence yelled. "We stand a chance up there."

The sub broke the surface and brought the creature with them. All eight of the things legs were wrapped around the hull, steadily stabbing away at it like a bird trying to crack a snail's shell.

"We need to get rid of it," Ian Young spoke to the captain.

"I am well aware of that, Lieutenant. I want three men armed and up top. If that thing wants to eat my sub, it can do it over my dead body." Captain Merriweather turned and walked away from the bridge. "You have control, Lieutenant."

Captain Merriweather met the three chosen members of his crew as they walked towards the hatch area. Together, the four of them climbed the rungs and popped the hatch. The thing's body curled around the sub. Its focus with the hull of the vessel proved to be its downfall as the four men opened fire, delivering a stream of rounds into the soft flesh of its undercarriage. The creature screamed and tried to turn, but it was too late. The hole the M16s had torn in its belly caused its insides to leak out of its body in a rush of thick black ink, which stunk like rotting fish.

"Good shooting, lads," Captain Merriweather proclaimed, just before his rifle fell against the hull of the boat, his arm still attached to mid-way along the forearm, at least.

Gunfire rang out in a deafening war cry and saw bullets bounce against the approaching creature that swam towards them, on long, thin tentacle whipping the air as it retracted.

"Brace, brace," a voice went up, and just a few hundred meters from the sub, the sea erupted in an explosion of water and sea monster flesh.

The wave from the blast crashed against the submarine which listed violently to the left, sending everybody overboard. The four men hit the water, sinking beneath the surface. The waiting tentacles wrapped around the bodies in an instant. The Kraken burst from the ground, enraged at being disturbed once more. Its hard shell opened and its mouth bloomed out from within.

Captain Merriweather made out the shadow in the dark and acted on instinct. He bit down into the limb that held him. His teeth tore through the soft flesh of the arm. He felt the gaping mouths of the suction cups tearing into his flesh, but he refused to give in without a fight. With his remaining arm, he clawed at the gash he had made. Chunks of black, bleeding flesh came away in his fingers. The grip around his body tightened. Clarence's lungs burned, his head was woozy from the blood he had lost. Not accounting for the multiple suction cup wounds that slowly deepened as the hungry pincers yanked his flesh from his body. Poison from the Kraken's blood swept through his body. It would have been a lethal dose, a painful death. Thankfully, Clarence Merriweather died before that moment came.

On the *Alaska*, the crew watched as the *Wyoming* rushed to the surface. They heard the gunfire and saw the second spider creating coming in from the blind side.

The decision to fire a torpedo so close to another submarine carried risks. While far from being an easy decision to make, Captain Douglas did so without hesitation.

He fired as far away as he dared, knowing that any impact would see off the creature, and the least he could do would be to give the *Wyoming* as much of a chance as possible.

With his attention focused on saving the *Wyoming,* Douglas and his crew did not notice the Kraken that lay buried beneath them.

The beast burst from the ocean, its cavernous outer shell slicing the *Wyoming* in two. Captain Douglas was too stunned to react. The order to fire came from his XO. Lieutenant Regal ordered the weapons officer to unload everything they had on the beast.

The sub shook from the rapid rate of fire, but within moments of each other, the five remaining torpedoes in the *Alaska's* stock were fired.

"Turn us around, we need to fall back. Get me in touch with the *Lassen*," Captain Douglas roared, his moment of hesitation a thing of the past.

"Good work, Lieutenant." The praise was more than Stuart had expected, or even hoped for.

***

Ian Young shook his fist in triumph as the spider creature was blown apart. He joined in the cheers, but was silenced as the sub got rocked by the torpedo explosion. The warning came too late. The crew was sent flying, and alarms began to blare. Smoke and sizzling electronics became the primary source of panic on the ship, while the hull itself seemed to groan from the sudden attack.

"Sir, she's here." The words were the final ones spoken on the ship, for in the next instant, the craft was shorn in two. Everything slowed, giving Ian enough time to look his crew in their eyes.

The water was cold, a fact which struck Ian as odd, but there was no time to dwell on the issue. Ian and the rest of those on the bridge were crushed in the initial rush. The two halves were enveloped by tentacles, which crushed the remains like aluminium cans, and discarded them to the ocean.

***

The group on board the *Lassen* stood by helpless as the Kraken tore apart the *Wyoming*. Forrest called for them to stay back. Emotions had run high during the moment, but his cooler, outsider perspective prevailed. They were too far away to do anything other than become fuel for the beast.

They needed to play it smart, and that was not going to happen if they charged in head first and swinging for the fences.

Captain Morgan wept for the losses, but was buoyed somewhat when she heard that the *Alaska* had survived. This was tempered by the news she had used her entire supply of torpedoes, which meant the sub would be useless in combat. However, three vessels meant they had another side covered for when the fight came.

As the senior officer among the CO's in the crippled attack group, Lisa Morgan found herself in charge of the show. She was used to the pressure, but she would be lying if she said the conditions under which it had happened did not add a certain weight on her soul.

"I think we need to call in some reinforcements," Jenna Harrington spoke.

"What do you have in mind, Lieutenant?" the master chief of the Coast Guard asked.

"We call in some choppers. We get those birds laying down fire from the skies. Distract that bitch for a while. Then we just sit back and hit the whore with everything we've got. I'm talking the big guns here." Jenna stood up moved over to the display screens. "We have the island here, we can slingshot the birds around, laying down fire as they come in. When they swing around, we launch the strikes from here, they come out from behind the island with all guns blazing, and high-tail it out of there before the harpoons hit. Heck, the Tomahawks if we need them."

Nobody disputed the logic or the plan, and so the ships kept their distance, and waited, hoping that the *Alaska* would reach them in time.

Meanwhile, the call was made back to Mayport, where Captain Henderson of the Coast Guard was brought up to speed on the plan. Four helicopters were scrambled, two from the Naval fleet and two from the Coast Guard.

CHAPTER 23

"What the fuck are those people doing?" Chester Williams spoke a little too loud, as the SeaHawk flew low over the beach before making a sharp turn out to sea.

"Check your words, Lieutenant," Roger McAllister growled.

"Sorry, Captain," Chester answered. "I just don't get why these people are standing around waiting for this monster to come and get them."

"They are curious, Lieutenant. I mean, we are talking about a genuine sea monster here. How often do you get the chance to see something like that?" Roger answered, throwing a smile towards his gunner.

"Not very many, because we're gonna blow this fucker out of the water," the lieutenant said with a cheer.

"Damned straight." Roger nodded and pull their bird up into the air.

Behind them, three others followed, each one armed to the teeth with Hellfire missiles and orders to shoot on sight.

"Gear up, fellas, we are five minutes out. They want us to come in hot and slingshot around the island. We are not there to be heroes today. We have a role to play, and we will do so to the best of our abilities," Roger said, relaying the instructions they had all been given before they took flight. "I want missiles screaming the moment that thing comes into range, and gunners, aim for the tentacles, I want to cripple that thing."

A round of agreements, whoops and hollers came back in response.

Not long later, the island came into view.

"Sir—" Chester began.

"I see it," Roger cut him off.

They all saw it.

**

Luke Stronghold grumbled as the *Gettysburg* returned to formation. His jaw was still ringing from where the old captain had socked him. If

116

the man had not been dead, Douglas would have reported him and seen him thrown out of the Navy.

His rage simmered beneath the surface as he was forced to suffer the indignity of having his command semi stripped away from him. Given to a woman no less. The idea that a woman could possibly lead a ship was beyond absurd, in his eyes at least. Let them sign up, keep them quiet and happy, but to give them command was nothing more than a recipe for long-winded disaster as far as Luke was concerned.

He stood on the bridge, his arms folded, with a scowl on his face and a general air of thunder about his person. He remained still, forced into silence as Amanda instructed the crew to fall into formation.

"Running, we are running away," Stronghold called to her. He was acting out, like the spoiled child he was.

"We are following orders, Captain," Amanda replied, not turning around from her station by the captain's chair to give him so much as a dismissive glare.

"Of course you are," Stronghold replied snidely.

The feeling on the bridge was one of awkwardness. There could be no avoided the tension that existed between the CO and his XO. Nobody wanted to interfere, but as a result, they did not know who to look at or what to say. So they kept their heads down, remained silent and simply carried out the duties that were assigned to them.

"Sir," a young and nervous voice called.

"Yes," both voices answered.

"We have something closing in. The creature ... it's ... chasing us," the technician announced.

"Sir, I have the *Lassen* on the wire. They are telling us to increase speed. We should stay in formation and lead the creature away," another voice spoke up.

"Jesus Christ," Luke growled. "That thing will catch us in a matter of miles. We need to strike, blow this fucker out of the water and go home. This monster hunt is beyond ridiculous."

"Increase the ships speed, keep us lined up, but I want the torpedo tubes ready to fire if needed. Also, I want people on both guns on deck. Anything moves, we shoot." Amanda stood her ground, but understood that there was a danger in just turning to run.

"Yes, sir," voices called out in acknowledgement of the order they were given.

The battered group led the creature away from the island, leading her into the path of the approaching helicopters.

"Sir, the creature is gaining on us, moving in at twenty-five knots," the sonar operator called out.

"What are you going to do, Amanda?" Luke asked, a smarmy grin plastered on his face.

"Push us to full speed. Prepare the torpedoes, just in case," Amanda ordered, making her way across the bridge to Captain Stronghold.

"Very bold," Stronghold spat, smirking.

"Listen, Captain, I am sorry about what happened, but I was given command of this ship, and you will be well served to remember that." Amanda tried to keep her voice steady as she stood up to the man who had made her life hell for so long.

"Take your moment, Amanda, enjoy it. I guarantee you there will not be another." Luke lowered his voice and glared at the woman before him.

"Screw you, Captain. Get off my bridge, now," Amanda roared, her blood boiling.

The open hand came out of nowhere. The flesh of her cheek burned, and the taste of blood tainted the back of her throat before Amanda really understood what had happened.

Silence swept over the bridge as Captain Stronghold gave a roar. He grabbed Amanda by her hair and pulled her close to him. "The *Gettysburg* is my ship, Amanda, my command, and I will be god damned to see you run her into the ground." His temper flared and a closed fist broke the XO's nose with a wet splat.

"Sirs," the panicked shout went up, just as the boat was rocked by a shot as hard as a torpedo strike. The glass of the bridge shattered as the thick, slimy limbs of the Kraken burst through. The walls groaned and burst as the thick arms filled the bridge and hauled the ship of out of the water.

The tentacle filled the bridge. Screams rang out as members of the crew were crushed by the weight of the giant limb, which continued to push its way into the cabin.

Amanda threw herself to the floor as the limb passed over her head. The ship listed as the tentacles wrapped around the hull and hauled the vessel into the air, and held the way a child would hold a toy car. The boat was swept through the air as the Kraken moved through the water. More screams filled the craft. Blood flooded the floor and flowed under Amanda, who was trying to claw her way over the steep incline of the bridge to possible safety.

The door to the main hall was open. It gave Amanda a focus and direction, and as she hauled her battered body over the metal floor, all she could think about was survival.

Her route was blocked however when the two fresh limbs appeared, probing their way through the ship in search of anything that would offer them sustenance.

Tears formed in Amanda's eyes as the realization came that her role in the war was over. Their fight was lost, but she would not go down on her arse. Her grandfather had always taught her that everybody and everything comes with an expiration date. The end is inevitable, but what is not, is how we choose to meet that end.

Adjusting her position, Amanda crawled under the stinking, pulsating main tentacle and inched her way over to the comms console. She hoped that there were still others alive on the ship.

A violent rattle swept through the vessel as the Kraken adjusted its position once more, raising the craft even further. Amanda was thankful that she did not have a view of what was going on.

The shudder pushed her back on the floor. Instinctively, she reached to find purchase, grabbing the tentacle for support. The thing reacted to her touch, twisting until the suction cup was facing her. Amanda stifled a horrified scream as the rubbery flesh unfurled and set after set of dripping pincers emerged, snapping at the air. They wiggled back and forth, snatching at anything they could reach, pulling and pushing their find towards its center, where a circular mouth sat puckered and waiting.

Amanda held in her scream, throwing herself flat against the floor, praying that the creature could not see or sense her. When nothing grabbed her, Amanda made her move again. She reached the console and rose to her knees, a task that was more difficult that she anticipated. Her left leg was broken, and her right was limp, numb to the touch and stained crimson with blood.

Groping, she hit the comms button and called out for anybody.

"Aye, Captain. I'm still alive," the gravelled voice of Jock McCoy came back. He was the ships senior most weapons officer, and the toughest son of a gun Amanda had ever met. He was also the nicest, a doting father to his children and grandchildren.

"I'm sorry, Jock," Amanda wept, unable to hold back the tears.

"Don't be, lass. We all have to meet our end at some point or another," the old man answered, his voice a perfect calm.

The ship groaned as the tentacles continued to fill the hallways, stretching the rivets and joints to their breaking point.

"Jock, I want you to fire all torpedoes, If this bitch is going to kill us, then we are going to make sure we give her some heartburn for her troubles," Amanda spoke with conviction, ignoring the new pain that erupted from her, the same way the two proving tentacles erupted from her body. One had speared her through the chest, and the other her gut. Blood spurted over the console in this thick, steaming spurts.

"Will do, lass. It was a pleasure sailing with you. God speed." Jock's voice went silent as the communications system failed. Not that Amanda heard him, for her still-warm corpse was already being broken down and forced through the large suction mouth of the main tentacle.

The ship shuddered as the torpedoes were fired, five in all were jettisoned at the beast, all of which found their mark.

***

"Would you look at that," Lieutenant Regal said with a whistle.

"That woman had guts and balls larger than mine," Captain Douglas said as he bowed his head momentarily as a sign of respect. "We need to keep moving. That thing is faster than us, and I do not want to meet my end that way."

The statement was a shared sentiment, and nobody argued about pushing the sub to maximum speed. Communication with *Lassen* was not needed, because she had also increased her speed and was making her way out into deep water.

"Sir, should we take her beneath the water?" Regal asked the captain.

"No, I don't see the point at the moment. The choppers are inbound, and I have a suspicion this bitch is even more deadly underwater," Douglas answered, hoping he sounded like a man confident in his choices. In truth, he was scared, and did not want to die.

***

Roger McAllister stared at the creature as two thick tentacles raised the *Gettysburg* into the air, snapping the cruiser in two with a simple twist of its massive limbs.

"God rest their souls," he said, making the sign of the cross as he angled the attack group of Seahawks towards the beast. "I want that gun roaring the second we come into range, Lieutenant."

"Yes, sir," Chester snapped his answer. A few seconds later, the M240 began to scream its war cry.

The four choppers moved from their diamond formation into a straight line, splitting two to the left and two to the right. One of each group went up high, and the other swept down low, spitting a collective total of four thousand rounds a minute at the creature.

Flesh exploded, and black blood fell in a rain storm as the flailing tentacles swallowed the first wave of fire.

"Incoming!" McAllister screamed as the Kraken launched both halves of the *Gettysburg* at the helicopters.

The four birds easily avoided the hurled remains, and united once again to launch a second wave of gunfire.

Three tentacles were severed and fell into the water, crashing down like falling buildings.

The beast sank beneath the waves, disappearing in an instant, leaving the helicopters with no target. Rather than swing around the island, they made a tighter turn, hoping to come around and catch the creature as it rose.

For a moment during their turn, the helicopters were blind, and a moment was all the time the Kraken needed to rise from the water, its hardened shell bursting open as it broke the surface. The force of its rising created a swell of water in every direction. Tentacles shot out and swatted two of the SeaHawks out of the sky with ease. The tail of one of the helicopters was sliced through, leaving the fuselage of the craft to crash into the ocean in a wild spiral. The second had a split second in which to react, and the slicing tentacle missed the tail, instead slicing through the main rotor blades. The chopper burst into flames and exploded, obliterating the limb at the same time.

In the lead bird, McAllister was just coming around as the second chopper went down. He pulled his machine into a steep climb to avoid the debris from the blast, and launched two Hellfire missiles in a quick counter strike. He pulled his machine around instantly, the notion of making a slingshot around the island was dead in the water. The missiles buried into the meaty flesh of the beast's gaping face and detonated with enough force to sink anything out on the water.

The meat bubbled like melting plastic, expanding as the blast was initially absorbed by its body. The bubble swelled and burst, sending oily blood shooting into to the air like an unplanned strike on a drilling rig.

The Kraken screamed and roared, its remaining tentacles flapping at its burning face. Sinking beneath the waves once more, injured and running for its life.

***

"Take us down," Captain Douglas bellowed his order as the wall of water surged towards them.

The submarine began to slip beneath the waves, but there was not enough time. The rush hit them, and shook the crew around like dolls.

"I want a damage report," Captain Douglas called, as he hauled himself to his feet.

"We are all clear, sir. We got shook up some, but everything seems functional still," a rather shaken-sounding voice came back.

"What about the *Lassen*?" Douglas asked.

"She is still there, but I'm hearing that she has problems. The wave hit her side on, they took a lot of damage," his XO replied.

"Damn it to Hell!" Douglas snarled slapping his fist against the nearest console unit.

"Sir, the creature has gone under," the sonar technician called. The man was sporting a lump on his head the size of a tennis ball, but had pulled himself back into position.

"Do we have anything left to defend ourselves with?" Douglas answered, all out of ideas.

"No, sir, but looks as though she is moving away from us," the man replied.

"We've got this motherfucker on the ropes. Tell the *Lassen* to ready its missiles," Douglas called, a surge of hope swelling in his gut.

***

"We've lost all power in the engines," the engineers called from the *Lassen*'s engine room. "This old girl can't keep taking hits like that."

"I understand, just get us moving any way you can. We cannot afford to be sitting ducks out here," Captain Morgan replied as she turned around to take stock of the damage her ship had suffered.

The wave had hit them on the broadside and came close to tipping the vessel completely. The bridge was a mess of broken glass, sea water, sparking computer terminals and buzzing alarms. Her sonar technician and communications officer were lying dead on the floor. The others on the bridge hauled themselves back to their feet, albeit barely.

Her XO had dislocated her shoulder but refused to abandon her position, and from the preliminary round of checks, the medical bay was not answering any of the messages they were being sent.

"Captain, we have a fire out on deck," one of the off-duty officers called out as they ran onto the bridge.

"Where?" Lisa Morgan asked.

"In the hangars. The helos were not fully stowed. The blast of the wave shook them loose, and they went up in flames. We've got everything under control, but we … we lost a lot of folks." The man hung his head as he spoke.

In the midst of all of the warnings list and sirens from the damaged ship, the proximity alarm that sounded to alert them of an incoming threat began to blare, but was lost to the general din of panic.

The Kraken was upon them before anybody had the chance to react.

The head emerged from the water between the *Alaska* and the *Lassen.* It rose the way anybody would expect a giant sea monster to rise. The head emerged smoothly from the water, the hardened shell gone, fallen away as a result of the hellfire strike. The flesh was red and angry, with black blood running in wide rivulets over the body.

"Captain, the Kraken …" Heather Watson cried out, but the first tentacle smashed against the side of the vessel cutting off her warning.

Also on the bridge were Forrest, Randolph, and Pete. There was no time for them to brace themselves for the impact. As a result, the three men had also been sent flying.

Forrest was on his feet, blood flowing from a deep head wound, while Randolph was limping, standing with his left arm wrapped around his midsection, clasping against his ribs.

Pete was lying on the floor, his right leg turned almost one hundred and eighty degrees in contrast to the rest of his body. He was still unconscious from his fall, which was a stroke of luck, because he also had a nasty wound on his chest, which had already stained his shirt dark red.

The assaulting tentacle slid through the shattered bridge window, pausing every so often, as if testing the air, like a snake. It approached the lifeless body of a nameless technician, a young seaman who had been standing near the window when the wave hit. His body had been torn apart by the shower of glass that was sent his way from the exploding window.

The tentacle brushed the body, sweeping over the lifeless flesh. The greedy suction sound that rose from the pulsing limb as hungry mouths sampled the scarlet liquid was enough to turn their stomachs.

Forrest looked around. A fire axe hung on the wall, the glass casing already shattered, the weapon sat waiting to be used.

The hungry tentacle moved away from the dead seaman and began to creep towards the unconscious Pete.

Moving fast as his weakening legs allowed, Forrest grabbed the weapon and turned around. The tentacle had already wrapped around Pete's body, sliding under and looping over his throat. They heard the crisp snap of hungry jaws biting fresh flesh. Pete's eyes sprang open. He stared around him, held frozen in panic. He opened his mouth to scream, but nothing came out.

Forrest stood with the axe raised, when a hand fell on his shoulders. Randolph spun the man around, mouthing instructions for Forrest to stop.

They were not under attack. The Kraken was exploring them, searching. They were not out of the woods, but to attack the creature in hand-to-hand combat would mean their certain death.

Two more tentacles entered the bridge, searching the space. They brushed over the bodies of the dead. Captain Morgan and her XO stood with their backs pressed against the far wall.

After a few moments, the tentacles tensed and withdrew. Outside, the Kraken was turning its attention to the submarine that had re-surfaced.

"Captain, captain, I've got the engines back online," the engineer called through the speakers. "They are not going to hold long, and we can't push them too fast, but there should be enough left to limp us home."

The *Lassen* sat too close the beast to make a break for freedom, and so the news was less than encouraging, yet Captain Morgan was determined to not let it show.

"That is good news, but I have another idea," Captain Morgan spoke in a whisper, unsure as to whether the creature could hear them, or would respond to the radio frequencies in any way,

The captain quickly and concisely explained her idea to the engineer, never breaking eye contact with her XO. Over the years, they had shared many moments, and Lisa Morgan was damned sure she would not make a decision without the backing of her second-in-command.

Heather Watson listened, focusing on the words and not the pain coursing through her upper body. She did her best to nod when the need arose. The prospect terrified her down to her boots, but at the same time, she understood that they had no other options left.

"Yes, sir, I will let you know when I am done," the engineer spoke solemnly. His professionalism overpowered his natural survival instinct.

***

The *Alaska* rose to the surface short of the creature. Inquisitive tentacles brushed over its hull. They ran along the metal curves, inspecting every access possibility, prodding the sub the way a cat toys with a dead mouse.

"Sir, what do we do?" Lieutenant Regal asked, his knees shaking as he struggled to control himself.

All around the sub, people held their breath. They could trace the tentacles movements over the hull, hear the scraping of the metal, and feel the pressure the limbs exerted.

"Get me the *Lassen*," Captain Douglas ordered, his face grim.

A few moments later, Lisa Morgan's voice came through the comms unit. She was whispering, at the very least speaking in hushed tones.

"We have minimal power, and I have my engineer rerouting everything to the missile launch controls." She was direct in her speech, not caring to waste any time on trivial discussions.

"A blast from such close range would—" Captain Douglas began.

"I know. I understand the risks, but I do not see any other choice. We are still and you are out of weapons," the experienced captain cut him off.

Lance Douglas said nothing for a while; his opposite number was right.

"What do you need us to do?" If they wanted to survive, then they all had a role to play.

"I need you to run block. Dive down, full speed ahead and head back out. I have the birds in the air coming back for a final run too." Lisa had everything planned out, and in the final moments, in their first real conversation, Douglas gained an immeasurable amount of respect for the *Lassen's* captain.

Douglas turned and addressed his helmsman. "I want us down deep, take us under this bitch and out the other side."

"Sir, she will tear us apart," the helmsman said, voicing his protestations.

"You just worry about taking us down. Let me worry about keeping us alive," Douglas answered, even managing a wry smile.

Grabbing the phone, the captain let out a long, deep breath as he waited for the weapons officer to answer.

"Flood the tubes." He gave the order immediately, giving himself no time to reconsider his actions.

"Sir?" the weapons officer asked.

"We need to buy the *Lassen* some time. We are going to circle around and move under the creature. I want to hit this fucker with some water slugs. After all, we don't have anything else left." Captain Douglas was no longer the same man he was when they left port that morning.

Having seen and suffered through more than many captains see in their whole career, he understood the difference between doing the right thing and doing the sensible thing. He wished he could have been able to see Captain Merriweather just one last time, even if just to shake his hand.

"Yes, sir, you give the order, and we will be ready," the weapons officer answered.

The mood on the sub was sombre as the ship drove its way to the seabed. The creature was right above them, occupied by the two remaining SeaHawks.

***

"Fire!" Roger McAllister roared as he brought his helo down towards the beast. The Kraken stared at them, an enormous eye appeared on the side of his face. A double layer of covering lids pulled back to reveal the orange glare of its fury.

Chester opened fire without returning a confirmation. He had just slammed in a fresh belt and smiled as the M240 thundered in his grip. The pulsating drum of its rapid fire was comforting, the continual spray of thick black blood was satisfying.

Chester was a great shot, and severed not one but two limbs as the primary helo pulled up and over the creatures head. Behind them, the second helicopter swept in and unleashed a volley of fire into the raw meat of the Kraken's head. The final strafe of fire tore through the giant eyeball, which exploded in a shower of dark red fluid. The fluid looked like blood, but given the copious volume of blackened sludge that had been shed from the beast's severed limbs, the red fluid had to be something else.

"Good shooting, now let's book," McAllister spoke as he turned away from the beast.

The Kraken howled in agony. The rage of its previous shrieks was gone, beaten into submission by a new sensation, one it did not understand, but felt in a pure way. The beast was in pain, and had nowhere left to run.

A large tentacle slapped out lazily as the second helo moved into its escape run. The SeaHawk easily evaded the clumsy limb.

In the water, something rumbled. A sensation the Kraken had felt before. In a swift movement, readying to use the last amounts of energy it could muster, the beast prepared to fight.

***

Captain Douglas head the news of the SeaHawk strike and swallowed hard. The time had come, his moment had arrived. The *Alaska*'s torpedo tubes were flooded with water, and they were ready to give the Kraken a true submariner's welcome.

"Sir, we are directly beneath the creature," the sonar technician whispered.

"Fire the first slug," Captain Douglas gave the order, his voice also not much more than a whisper.

The submarine shook as the torpedo tube pushed its contents back out into the ocean. The rush created a thick stream of bubbles, and a burst of noise designed to distract the creature shot from the rear of the vessel.

"Sir, we have movement," the pale-faced sonar technician called.

"Fire the second tube." Douglas clapped his hands together in defiance of the beast.

"I don't think—" the technician began, but was never able to finish.

The sub shook as the second torpedo tube emptied. Only, unlike the first shot, the *Alaska* did not stop shaking. The rumble became a tremor, and then suddenly, everything stopped. The submarine gave a groan and the walls began to implode.

"Sir, the creatures, she's … she's got us." Panic filled the sub, as the walls were crushed by the giant tentacle that wrapped around them.

"I want full power, this bitch won't get us without a fight," Douglas roared, as he grabbed hold of the nearest console. The submarine shuddered as the engines grumbled onwards to maximum capacity. The move only seemed to infuriate the beast, whose grip tightened even further. The walls of the bridge buckled inwards, and the tap, tap, tapping of the hungry suction cups shot through the walls.

"It's got us tight, we can't break free," the chief engines officer grunted, the stress of his attempts to save them heavy on his voice.

"Fire two more slugs," Douglas ordered.

"Sir, we didn't refill the tubes, you never—" The voice was drowned out but the screeching sound of crushed metal. The line went dead.

Lance Douglas stood up straight and looked around. The battle was lost.

"I hope the *Lassen* can take its shot," Regal spoke as he braced himself against the same console his CO was using.

"You and I both, Lieutenant, you and I both."

***

"Captain, we have lost contact with the *Alaska*. She fired something at the beast while she was beneath the thing, but now there is no sign of her." The announcement was not one that made Lisa Morgan smile. For all of his stubbornness, Lance Douglas was a fine captain, and his crew was first rate.

"This bitch has cost us everything," the captain spoke to her bridge. Picking up the receiver, Lisa called through to the weapons officer. "I want to have two Tomahawks in the air on my command."

"Captain, we are too close, a blast like that would destroy us." Randolph took the opportunity to speak up.

"I understand your concern, Captain, but this vessel is dead in the water. We won't be around long enough for backup to arrive, and I will not go down without a fight." Randolph recognized the conviction in the captain's words. There would be no reasoning with the captain, her resolve only strengthened as her fear shrank away. As much as Randolph wished for the contrary, they were out of options.

The Kraken rose from the water, its tentacles floating on the surface. It did not have much strength left, and sat on the surface, not moving, resting. The *Alaska* was gone, crushed down to a lump of iron the size of a family hatchback and buried in the seabed.

Lisa Morgan, and all of those on the bridge, stared at the creature. With the toughened outer shell removed, the real body of the beast was soft and fleshy. Its one remaining eye opened, but it never focused on the ship. The giant body shuddered, whether in an attempt to draw breath or as a result of the injuries the beast had sustained, they neither knew nor cared.

"Ma'am, I think …" Heather began.

"Fire." The captain gave the order and a few moments later, the ship lurched violently as the two Tomahawk missiles were launched from its deck.

At the same time, the creature raised its main tentacle, which had floated beneath the *Lassen*. Slapping against the underside of the vessel, it launched the ship to one side in a vicious swipe. The slimy arm caught the destroyer and wrapped around her hull. The tip emerged on the far side of the deck only to come crashing down hard enough to dent to decks floor.

Screams and shouts echoed through the ship as people braced themselves for both an attack from the beast, and the blast from the two warheads they just fired.

The blast came with a rush of wind and an ear-splitting crack, like being caught in the middle of a thunderstorm, only not on the ground but in the air, just at the point where the thunder is created.

Fire filled the vision of everybody on the bridge, and suddenly the *Lassen* was airborne.

The force of the blast, and the snap of the Kraken's body as the detonating missiles tore the beast apart, hurled the ship away from immediate danger. Chunks of burning meat pounded the ocean's surface like meteors plummeting from space. They pounded the *Lassen's* deck as the damaged destroyer skimmed over the water like a stone thrown by a bored schoolboy. Everybody was thrown in every direction possible, bodies crashed into the walls, consoles and each other. Bones snapped, skin split and blood was shed, but the blasts died down, and the ocean calmed. With everything said and done, the *Lassen* remained afloat. Just.

The ship listed heavily to port, but with no systems left alive to give her any reports, Captain Morgan was left blind to the extent of the damage. The bridge was a mess. Bodies lay strewn, cradling broken limbs. Morgan's XO lay on the floor by the captain's feet. Her lifeless body twisted in ways no human body should ever bend. Blood pooled around her head which had been caved inward, as if her skull had melted.

"I'm sorry," Morgan sobbed. The death toll was heavy. The deck had been swept clean by the power of the blast and the rush of the boat's trajectory. The thing that remained was a large section of tentacle, which flapped about for a moment before falling still.

Three others were alive on the bridge, including Captain Randolph Wiseman; the toughened dog was broken and bruised, but very much alive. The same could not be said for Forrest. The old man lay with his neck broken, the fire axe still clamped in his grip.

Captain Morgan looked through the shattered remains of her bridge. The ocean was black; as far as she could see, the blood of the Kraken covered the water. Floating lumps of its obliterated body dotted the rolling surface like tiny meat icebergs.

Below the bridge, one of the deck doors burst open and several members of the crew emerged. They were bloodied and beaten, but most certainly alive, which gave Lisa's spirits a boost.

"We did it," Jenna Harrington spoke, hauling herself to her feet. Her ankle was broken, or at least not of my use. She leaned heavily on the nearest console, managing a smile that brought tears to her eyes.

"Yes … yes, we did," Lisa said, hobbling her way across the bridge and down to the rest of her crew. Jenna followed, leaning on the equally shaken but sure-footed Randolph.

The two SeaHawks lowered themselves as close to the *Lassen* as they dared and filled themselves with the surviving crew members.

Chuck abandoned his gun post, and along with the second gunner, Scott Carlson, they swept through the remains of the boat. Fully loaded, the helos took to the sky.

In spite of the bright blue, cloudless sky, and the increasing temperature of the day, the beaches were desolate. Not a soul was to be seen walking over the white sand.

Chuck thought about mentioning it, but one look at the battered souls he shared his chopper with, he thought better of it.

They had won. The fight had cost them a lot, but the Kraken was dead, and as always, life would go on. There would always be another war to be fought, another threat looming on the horizon. Yet, in spite of that, the beaches would refill, tourists and locals alike would return to the water, and the day would become one of legend. Everybody would remember where they were the day the Kraken rose.

The End

CHECK OUT OTHER GREAT DEEP SEA THRILLERS

THEY RISE
by Hunter Shea

Some call them ghost sharks, the oldest and strangest looking creatures in the sea.

Marine biologist Brad Whitley has studied chimaera fish all his life. He thought he knew everything about them. He was wrong. Warming ocean temperatures free legions of prehistoric chimaera fish from their methane ice suspended animation. Now, in a corner of the Bermuda Triangle, the ocean waters run red. The 400 million year old massive killing machines know no mercy, destroying everything in their path. It will take Whitley, his climatologist ex-wife and the entire US Navy to stop them in the bloodiest battle ever seen on the high seas.

SERPENTINE
by Barry Napier

Clarkton Lake is a picturesque vacation spot located in rural Virginia, great for fishing, skiing, and wasting summer days away.

But this summer, something is different. When butchered bodies are discovered in the water and along the muddy banks of Clarkton Lake, what starts out as a typical summer on the lake quickly turns into a nightmare.

This summer, something new lives in the lake...something that was born in the darkest depths of the ocean and accidentally brought to these typically peaceful waters.

It's getting bigger, it's getting smarter...and it's always hungry.

CHECK OUT OTHER GREAT DEEP SEA THRILLERS

SEA RAPTOR
by John J. Rust

From terrorist hunter to monster hunter! Jack Rastun was a decorated U.S. Army Ranger, until an unfortunate incident forced him out of the service. He is soon hired by the Foundation for Undocumented Biological Investigation and given a new mission, to search for cryptids, creatures whose existence has not been proven by mainstream science. Teaming up with the daring and beautiful wildlife photographer Karen Thatcher, they must stop a sea monster's deadly rampage along the Jersey Shore. But that's not the only danger Rastun faces. A group of murderous animal smugglers also want the creature. Rastun must utilize every skill learned from years of fighting, otherwise, his first mission for the FUBI might very well be his last.

OCEAN'S HAMMER
by D.J. Goodman

Something strange is happening in the Sea of Cortez. Whales are beaching for no apparent reason and the local hammerhead shark population, previously believed to be fished to extinction, has suddenly reappeared. Marine biologists Maria Quintero and Kevin Hoyt have come to investigate with a television producer in tow, hoping to get footage that will land them a reality TV show. The plan is to have a stand-off against a notorious illegal shark-fishing captain and then go home.

Things are not going according to plan.

There is something new in the waters of the Sea of Cortez. Something smart. Something huge. Something that has its own plans for Quintero and Hoyt.

CHECK OUT OTHER GREAT DEEP SEA THRILLERS

MEGATOOTH
by Viktor Zarkov

When the death rate of sperm whales rises dramatically, a well-respected environmental activist puts together a ragtag team to hit the high seas to investigate the matter. They suspect that the deaths are due to poachers and they are all driven by a need for justice.

Elsewhere, an experimental government vessel is enhancing deep sea mining equipment. They see one of these dead whales up close and personal...and are fairly certain that it wasn't poachers that killed it.

Both of these teams are about to discover that poachers are the least of their worries. There is something hunting the whales...

Something big
Something prehistoric.
Something terrifying.
MEGATOOTH!

BLOOD CRUISE
by Jake Bible

Ben Clow's plans are set. Drop off kids, pick up girlfriend, head to the marina, and hop on best friend's cruiser for a weekend of fun at sea. But Ben's happy plans are about to be changed by a tentacled horror that lurks beneath the waves.

International crime lords! Deep cover black ops agents! A ravenous, bloodsucking monster! A storm of evil and danger conspire to turn Ben Clow's vacation from a fun ocean getaway into a nightmare of a Blood Cruise!

CHECK OUT OTHER GREAT DEEP SEA THRILLERS

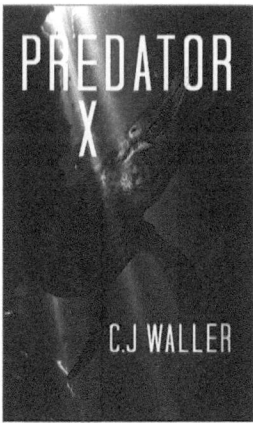

PREDATOR X
by C.J Waller

When deep level oil fracking uncovers a vast subterranean sea, a crack team of cavers and scientists are sent down to investigate. Upon their arrival, they disappear without a trace. A second team, including sedimentologist Dr Megan Stoker, are ordered to seek out Alpha Team and report back their findings. But Alpha team are nowhere to be found – instead, they are faced with something unexpected in the depths. Something ancient. Something huge. Something dangerous. Predator X

DEAD BAIT
by Tim Curran

A husband hell-bent on revenge hunts a Wereshark...A Russian mail order bride with a fishy secret...Crabs with a collective consciousness...A vampire who transforms into a Candiru...Zombie piranha...Bait that will have you crawling out of your skin and more. Drawing on horror, humor with a helping of dark fantasy and a touch of deviance, these 19 contemporary stories pay homage to the monsters that lurk in the murky waters of our imaginations. If you thought it was safe to go back in the water...Think Again!

CHECK OUT OTHER GREAT DEEP SEA THRILLERS

MEGA
by **Jake Bible**

There is something in the deep. Something large. Something hungry. Something prehistoric.
And Team Grendel must find it, fight it, and kill it.
Kinsey Thorne, the first female US Navy SEAL candidate has hit rock bottom. Having washed out of the Navy, she turned to every drink and drug she could get her hands on. Until her father and cousins, all ex-Navy SEALS themselves, offer her a way back into the life: as part of a private, elite combat Team being put together to find and hunt down an impossible monster in the Indian Ocean. Kinsey has a second chance, but can she live through it?

THE BLACK
by **Paul E Cooley**

Under 30,000 feet of water, the exploration rig Leaguer has discovered an oil field larger than Saudi Arabia, with oil so sweet and pure, nations would go to war for the rights to it. But as the team starts drilling exploration well after exploration well in their race to claim the sweet crude, a deep rumbling beneath the ocean floor shakes them all to their core. Something has been living in the oil and it's about to give birth to the greatest threat humanity has ever seen.

"The Black" is a techno/horror-thriller that puts the horror and action of movies such as Leviathan and The Thing right into readers' hands. Ocean exploration will never be the same."

CHECK OUT OTHER GREAT DEEP SEA THRILLERS

LAMPREYS
by Alan Spencer

A secret government tactical team is sent to perform a clean sweep of a private research installation. Horrible atrocities lurk within the abandoned corridors. Mutated sea creatures with insane killing abilities are waiting to suck the blood and meat from their prey.

Unemployed college professor Conrad Garfield is forced to assist and is soon separated from the team. Alone and afraid, Conrad must use his wits to battle mutated lampreys, infected scientists and go head-to-head with the biggest monstrosity of all.

Can Conrad survive, or will the deadly monsters suck the very life from his body?

DEEP DEVOTION
by M.C. Norris

Rising from the depths, a mind-bending monster unleashes a wave of terror across the American heartland. Kate Browning, a Kansas City EMT confronts her paralyzing fear of water when she traces the source of a deadly parasitic affliction to the Gulf of Mexico. Cooperating with a marine biologist, she travels to Florida in an effort to save the life of one very special patient, but the source of the epidemic happens to be the nest of a terrifying monster, one that last rose from the depths to annihilate the lost continent of Atlantis.

Leviathan, destroyer, devoted lifemate and parent, the abomination is not going to take the extermination of its brood well.

www.ingramcontent.com/pod-product-compliance
Lightning Source LLC
Chambersburg PA
CBHW020309150626
46552CB00022B/2260